JACK BE DEAD: REVELATION

JACK BE DEAD: REVELATION

STEPHEN DAVID BROOKS
JEFF LYONS

Storygeeks
Press

Jack Be Dead: Revelation

Copyright © 2016 by Stephen David Brooks & Jeff Lyons

ISBN: 978-0-9970663-0-2 (pbk)

ISBN: 978-0-9970663-1-9 (mobi)

ISBN: 978-0-9970663-2-6 (epub)

Cover art by Tracy Lyn

Interior design by Jeff Lyons

Give feedback on the book at:

feedback@storygeekspress.com

First Edition

Printed in the U.S.A

DEDICATION

This is for loyal readers past, present, and future.
Because without you, what's the point?

ACKNOWLEDGMENTS

Acknowledgments:

The authors would like to thank the following individuals for their support, help, encouragement, patience, infinite patience, faith, trust, belief, handouts, generosity, and small petty crimes undertaken to promote the success of this book.

• *Tracy Lyn* (www.virtuallypossibledesigns.com) thank you

for the amazing book cover designs and graphics.

• *Kimberley Heart, Deborah Calla, Mary Barr, Caroline Leavitt*—thank you for being trusted beta readers and telling us the truth.

• *Elinor Perry-Smith*—thank you for your keen eye and line edit.

ALSO BY JEFF LYONS

FICTION

Jack Be Dead: Revelation (bk #1)

13 Minutes

Terminus Station

NONFICTION

Anatomy of a Premise Line: How to Use Story and Premise
Development for Writing Success

Rapid Story Development: How to Use the Enneagram-
Story Connection to Become a Master Storyteller

Rapid Story Development: The Storyteller's Toolbox
Volume One

RAPID STORY DEVELOPMENT E-BOOK SERIES

#1: Commercial Pace in Fiction and Creative Nonfiction

#2: Bust the Top Ten Creative Writing Myths to Become a
Better Writer

#3: Ten Questions Every Writer Needs to Ask Before They
Hire a Consultant

#4: Teams and Ensembles: How to Write Stories with Large

Casts

CONTENTS

PROLOGUE

She loved the Dorchester. Her suite overlooked Park Lane, part of London's Inner Ring Road that runs from the south of Hyde Park Corner, north to the Marble Arch, dividing Hyde Park on the west side from Mayfair east. London's city lights sparkled like stars through the room's triple-glazed windows. *Triple glazed*, she thought with a little giggle. Most luxury hotels only use double glaze, but not the Dorchester; only the best for its customers. *It's the details that matter.* The opulence of the rooms was one thing, but the care paid to privacy—*That's what makes doing business here so magnificent.* Exterior walls faced with cork; floors and ceilings of the bedrooms and suites lined with compressed seaweed; all windows triple-glazed; luscious, sound-absorbing carpeting; and triple-thick, floor-to-ceiling draperies. She could be running chainsaws and no one would be any the wiser. *Brilliant.*

"Baby ..." his voice was weak, trembling, pleading.

Standing in front of the large, living room windows she sipped her vintage, 2004 Veuve Clicquot Brut, and ran her fingers over the thick, white, cotton bathrobe that moved across her naked body. Dark chestnut eyes contrasted with the flowing blonde hair that she kept in a stylish topknot, and her classic good looks could have easily belonged to a film siren, or a rock 'n roll bad girl. But, she was neither of those things; she had a higher calling.

Her client liked reveals. He liked the sight of her naked in red pumps, clad in a genuine Turkish bathrobe. The pumps and the bathrobe were always waiting for her when she entered the suite. Their ritual was well established after months of wooing. She was always first to arrive. After ordering chilled champagne and room service, she was to undress and then go into the bathroom, turn on the hot shower to steam the place into a proper London pea-souper, and then leave a pair of soiled panties in the bathroom for him to find —nothing gross, but stained enough to give a nice smell. Then she was to put on the shoes, then the robe, and then wait quietly in an anteroom. All this had to be done before his eleven p.m. arrival. And this she did, each time, every week, for three months.

"Please—fucking God in heaven—please ..." *Was he crying? Possibly.*

His part of the rite was more straightforward. Upon arrival he was to go straight to the bathroom, undress, indulge his fetish for women's underwear, and then take his place on the stool. It was a simple piece of furniture, pine wood about two feet high, placed in the center of the bathroom. Above him was a strong light fixture with a noose hanging from it. A pair of unlocked handcuffs hung from the open loop of the noose, and his job was to put the noose over his head, tighten it around his fleshy neck, and then put his hands behind his back where he was to lock the handcuffs in place. This all usually took twenty minutes, no more. And this he did, each time, every week, without fail.

And so tonight she danced her part; he danced his. Only, tonight was going to be different. He had probably figured that out by now, as she was usually bringing him to his happy ending by this point. He must have been standing on that stool, with that noose around his neck, for at least forty minutes, and at his age and physical condition he had to be feeling the pain. She finished off her champagne, gathered her robe tightly around her, and walked slowly to the bath-room. *Time for the big reveal.*

He hung from the ceiling, trembling and covered in sweat, wearing nothing but an old jockstrap. Middle-aged, balding, paunchy, and in no physical condition to handle anything more strenuous than a brisk walk up a flight of stairs, his bloodshot eyes were wide open and unblinking as they followed her as she moved across the bathroom to stand in front of him.

"I don't like... this game ... I ... can't ... stand ... much longer ..." he stammered.

"Just a bit longer, just for me, love?" In a flourish, she undid the bathrobe tie and threw back the cloth to stand naked before him. She thought his eyes were as wide as they could possibly be, given that he was close to hanging himself. But, no, they actually grew rounder at the sight of her.

"I think I should get down now!" he said, as his eyes locked on her red pumps. The stool tottered a bit with his unsteady legs, and then his gaze froze to hers.

"Come on, baby—fun's over." The veins in his neck throbbed and his face was flushed with blood, "I'll double your rate. Anything." She ignored him, walked over to a cabinet and pulled out an antique bag, the kind doctors once used to make house calls. "What's this bit? What's in that thing?" he asked.

"This old thing? It's my toolbox. It holds my tools." She switched into sex mode, set the bag on the floor, and walked in front of him. His jock was nearly eye-level to her mouth. She began to stroke him. He lost his footing and nearly fell. She saw the mixed emotions on his face: half terror, half ecstasy. But, the terror was clearly winning.

"Take me the fuck down! Now!" he ordered.

"Now, now Johnny. I don't think you're in a position to make demands." She ripped down his jockstrap with a violent tug, and gave him a blow job. She knew he would be soft; after all, what normal man could hold an erection with a noose tightening around his neck and death just one leg cramp away? Well—she knew of one man.

From some primitive, animal place deep within, he somehow found the strength to shout in a voice that echoed off the walls like a shockwave, "Help!" It was then she kicked the stool out from under him.

She stepped back quickly as his weight closed the noose. His arms struggled against the handcuffs, ripping the skin at his wrists. Reaching behind the bathroom door she pulled out a long, wide roll of plastic and hastily unrolled it out under his flailing legs. She knew there were only moments before his spine snapped and it would all be over. She also knew that when it was, he would piss and shit himself as his organs ripped and his sphincter muscles released. She didn't want the blood from his wrists and his shit staining the tile grout. It was going to be hard enough to sanitize the room when she was done.

She reached out to stop him from swinging beyond the edges of the plastic, and as she stilled him, his limp body let go with a flush of sludge. Even knowing what was coming, she was unprepared for the stench. She checked the floor for splatter and smiled. All clear. It was then she looked ahead and saw John's final gift to her: "angel lust." That was one of the names for it, along with "death erection," "terminal erection," or priapism. She remembered reading in one of her medical textbooks that hanging victims, both men and women, often experienced full genital arousal after being hanged. When pressure is exerted on the cerebellum by the noose, a penis can reach a full state of erection, accompanied by the forced discharge of urine, mucus, or prostatic fluid. In the Middle Ages, during public executions, women and young girls would clamor to be front and center at the gallows in the hope of seeing angel lust in all its glory. And if they were pious, and very good they might just get sprinkled with some angel dust. They had a one-in-three chance, because angel lust was present in one out of every three hangings. "Well, Johnny boy," she said out loud, "tonight, one-in-three is your lucky number."

She touched the hood of his cock and pulled it toward her with the tips of her fingers, and then let it go. It snapped back against his abdomen like a rubber band, "Time for work." She kicked off her pumps and knelt down beside the antique bag that had captured his earlier attention. She opened the bag and delicately removed surgical equipment: scalpels, saws, a hammer, and a tube of red lipstick. She removed the cap and in a couple of practiced strokes set her lips on fire.

After cleaning up the mess, she carefully maneuvered John's body to the floor and laid him out on the plastic sheet, face up. There was no hurry. She took her time. They had the room until the next day, with a late checkout. Rummaging through her bag, she pulled out an old iPod and headphones. Spinning the iPod's magic wheel, she found the perfect song to energize the hours that lay ahead, and soon a pulsing beat drowned out all noise, all thought, all distraction.

Looking at the array of blades lying on the floor, she instead reached back into her black bag and pulled out a shiny pair of pliers. She ran the tool lovingly down the entire length of John's hairy torso. But then her attention shifted. She knelt by the right side of his head and with one hand opened his mouth wide. Smiling, she reached inside and with some effort, gritting her own teeth a bit, she ripped out a tooth. Holding it up proudly she said, "He loves me ..." She laid it on the plastic gingerly.

Then she pulled out a second, "... he loves me not ..." and laid it next to the first tooth.

Then a third, "... he loves me ..." and continued in this way, with great care, being very methodical, and thinking to herself the whole time, *It's the details that matter*.

CHAPTER 1

Albert Valentine's childhood growing up on the working class streets of Birmingham taught him the meaning of survival. Consequently, he learned at an early age to always travel his own road, preferring the unknown fork to the familiar turn. His life reflected risk, always taken on his terms, but adventurous nonetheless. Someone who didn't know him would never suspect that underneath the black suit, white shirt, and black bow tie that he wore as a daily uniform, was a man capable of stacking bodies, and walking through fire. But, maybe those days were gone, did that Albert exist anymore? After sixty-six years on the planet, his hair was a mat of gray nap, his skin, especially around his eyes, wrinkled and weathered, and his once nimble and dexterous hands that had moved like a whirlwind were now swollen and arthritic. He felt he had earned some measure of peace, some modicum of amity with the world. Alas, the world did not seem to agree.

Albert wasn't a fraud, but he always felt like one. Even when it came to his second favorite activity, chess, he felt more the trickster than the chess master. Here at Holland Park, where he played every Sunday, he had a bit of a reputation for being aloof as a person, but formidable as a player. His opponents knew better than to pull cutesy openings, or flavor-of-the-month strategies with him. God save you if you tried a Fried Liver Attack, or the Sicilian Pterodactyl Variation, or the Hippopotamus Defense. A serious player's only chance to beat Albert was to stick to classical lines, the more complicated the better: Giuoco Piano, London System, French Defense, or the King's or Queen's Indian Defenses. This was why he was formidable, and this Albert liked.

The aloof moniker was earned because he hated shaking his opponent's hands. He did it because it was expected; shaking hands was part of the ritual of chess. But, what he did could hardly be called a handshake: fingertips and thumbs barely grabbing and then instantly releasing. Anyone receiving such a handshake would have to feel his effort was less than sincere. Did he—Albert—do this to provoke them so they would play more aggressively? Did he do it to make them feel diminished, or unimportant, and thus unsettle them before the first move was even played? Or did he just not give a damn?

Albert knew this was what went on in the heads of his opponents, but he also knew it was all bunk. But, they insisted on touching, being polite, sportsman-like. And this was the reason for feeling like a cheat. As soon as Albert touched his opponents he knew their moves, their plan of action, the variations they prepared to play, and their blind spots and positional foibles. All from a touch. It had always been this way, always feeling the cheat.

All his life he tried to be careful, respectful of others, to allow everyone their three feet of personal space. He remembered reading about the "space thing" in some pop-psych magazine years earlier, while on a trip to the Magic Castle in Los Angeles, California. Albert had been invited by the Castle to perform his famous dove act. Albert was "the dove guy." That's all he did, when he performed public magic, make birds appear and disappear, while being assisted by buxom, knock-down-gorgeous assistants. But, Albert's act was not just some guy pulling doves out of a hat. He had style, panache, theatrics, emotion. Magicians would come from miles around just to watch his hands move. Even the professionals could not figure out how he could create a theatrical event based on evaporating birds. *That's why they call it magic.*

Being invited to be the headline act at the Magic Castle was a major feather in Albert's professional cap. As a member of London's prestigious magician's society the Magic Circle, he had performed all over the United Kingdom and Ireland, and across the European Union, but never in the United States. Being invited into the Castle's Academy of Magical Arts was a rare privilege, almost as rare as an American being invited into the Circle's inner sanctum. The rivalry was friendly, but serious. Albert recalled standing in front of the Magic Castle's châteauesque façade and admiring the ornate turn-of-the-century opulence, and remembering that London's own Magic Circle was founded in 1905, four years earlier than the Magic Castle. Somehow that mattered to Albert at the time, his British pride swelling at the thought, *We're older and better.*

But that night at the Castle was destined to be special in ways Albert would have never anticipated. Through some unknown mechanism, or random act of nature, he must have shorted a circuit, or crossed some internal psychic wiring, because a nuisance that had pestered him all his life, from childhood right through his lamentable years at King's College, Oxford, suddenly went haywire and Albert found himself psychically connected to every tourist, magician, and waiter in the place.

As soon as he touched someone he knew their intentions, their immediate plans, their emotional states, but most disturbing of all he could see into their histories. He had always been "sensitive," able to sense people's emotions and even some of their intentions, and over the course of his life he'd grown comfortable with these inklings, trusting himself enough to know they were right and true, and not delusions or fantasies. He managed them, like a chronic illness; he had always been in control of his sensations, never the other way around. And yes, as with Holland Park, he'd used his limited abilities to gain some leverage in school when the going got tough, or to talk his way out of fights with bullies in the school yard, and even once to outguess one of his professors at King's, but those experiences were never as physically powerful as that night at the Castle.

That night he nearly went mad touching his fellow magicians and seeing exactly how every trick and illusion was going to be performed. He sensed five men who were going to leave their wives, nine women who were cheating on their husbands, some with each other, and one dark soul who was planning a murder. This person just bumped him slightly, and then disappeared into the crowd and Albert could not find him again to do anything about it, but he knew someone in that building would be dead the next morning.

Knowing an innocent person was going to die, and not being able to do anything about it was disturbing enough, but it was this new-found ability to see back into personal timelines that threw him into a panic. Men, women, children—everyone he touched was older than he could imagine. He'd heard about past lives, but until this moment they had just been stories. Now, he saw them, felt them, was inside them. They were just fleeting moments, but they were as real as any he had experienced in his own life.

As he fled from the Castle in a terror that night, and stood alone in the chilly Los Angeles air, the voices receded, and the images blurred, but he was never himself again. He had been changed, but by what he did not know.

That's why he was in Holland Park, on this day, not to play chess, but to get answers. For months Albert had been "seeing" things, not just in dreams at night, but also walking around in the normal course of his day. And, unlike his Magic Castle experience, he didn't have to be touching someone for the "seeing" to occur.

Gestalts of awareness, memories, frightening tableauxes of images; some ancient, some current, all disjointed and disconnected, would randomly flash into his mind. He knew in his deepest self that nothing was random, everything was connected, and these connections would eventually clarify, but in the meantime his frustration was that the visions were more like impressions, not really images, with powerful emotions attached. Unlike the impressions, however, the emotions were clear: fear, dread, horror, revulsion. He and his family were in danger, but he had no idea from what or from whom. Something was coming, something old with rage that ran deeper than any ocean, and it knew his name. And so, Albert made the call. It was a phone call he said he would never make, to the one person he said he would never see alive on this Earth again. If two people were ever destined to strangle one another for the sheer joy of committing bloody murder, then they were Albert and the man who was walking toward him through the Holland Park cafe and into the chess patio.

Lord Alistair Franklin was the former president of the Magic Circle, Britain's premiere society for professional magicians. He was also the man single-handedly responsible for ending Albert's professional life as a magician. It was Lord Franklin who paid the costs of Albert's expulsion from the Circle out of his own pocket, and for the subsequent campaign of character assassination that followed. When it was all done, Albert couldn't get a get a job doing magic at a kid's party, let alone a major club or public venue. It had been over a decade since the men last spoke civilly to one another, and even longer since they could tolerate being in the same room together.

Lord Franklin was an archetype of the stuffy Tory, complete with country estates, Irish wolfhounds, and despite the toothless government ban on the practice, the occasional Boxing Day fox hunt. He was all pomp and circumstance, Cuban cigars, and harbored a not-so-secret passion to be named a Knight of the Order of the Garter. Lord Franklin had the pedigree for, if hardly the record of, civic service to the Crown to warrant such an honor. And, being a practicing master magician didn't win him any high marks with his old-boy cronies in the House of Lords, who regarded professional magicians one rung up from taxi drivers.

All of that was more than enough for Albert to justifiably write off Lord Franklin as an insufferable and unendurable human being, save for Alistair's one saving grace: he was also gifted with the same clairvoyant talents as Albert, although Lord Franklin was always better at hiding his truer self behind an upper-crust persona.

It was an odd paradox that gifted individuals, such as the two men, could read other people's psychic states, and even have the occasional premonition, but were entirely incapable of doing the same for themselves as individuals. Albert, for all practical purposes, was as blind as a mole when it came to his own psychic process. If he wanted to "get read" he'd have to find another clairvoyant, someone of similar talent and psychic strength.

Lord Franklin stepped up to the chess table where Albert sat, and looked down on him accusingly. It was an awkward silence, but a short one.

"Hello Albert," he said. Alistair sat down, "You'll forgive me if we don't shake hands."

"Hello Alistair, thank you for coming."

"Albert, you look terrible," he smiled, "I hope you don't mind me saying so."

Albert returned a snide grin, "Of course not. I haven't been sleeping well."

"Oh, I am sorry. Crippling guilt? Haunted by the past? It does catch up, doesn't it?" Lord Franklin grinned.

Albert was prepared for a certain amount of snark,

but clearly this was going to be intolerable, "I don't want to fight with you."

"Really? Then we should have met over an espresso, not a chessboard. The metaphor is a bit thick, even for you."

"As I said on the phone, I need your help. Your particular kind of help," Albert said.

Lord Franklin paused for a long time, drumming his fingers on the molded concrete table, "Yes, so you said. I must say that I was truly confused to get your call. After what happened between us, I would have thought I'd be the last person you would have called."

Albert interrupted him, annoyed, "Then why did you agree to meet me?"

"You sounded ..." Lord Franklin chose his words carefully, "... well, desperate."

"I guess you don't have to be a bloody psychic to figure that out, eh?" Albert almost laughed.

"I killed your career, I expelled you from the society, and I turned my back on a decades-long friendship," Lord Franklin said, "I figured I owed you one."

"Crippling guilt? Haunted by the past?" Albert countered.

Lord Franklin smiled contritely and took a deep breath, "You left us no choice, Albert. You left me no choice."

"You had choices!" There was a stubbornness in Albert's voice, like he was digging in his heels.

"You still think you were the injured party. Thank you for reminding me why I disowned you." Lord Franklin let Albert have it, "You gave people up! You stood in public demonstrations—I was there—and exposed other magicians' techniques. You violated our most sacred code, *indocilis privata loqui*, remember?"

"Incapable of speaking private things," replied Albert, "Yes, I remember."

"Yes! You not only spoke private things, you gave out the damn details. Do you know how many members wanted to sue you into the workhouse? I stopped them. No, no, don't thank me!" Lord Franklin chided. He was on his high horse, but Albert wasn't so sure he didn't have a right to be, "What you did was the magician's equivalent to giving away state secrets. Nothing less than treason!"

"Punishable by death?" Albert asked.

"In a perfect world," Lord Franklin replied making one last dig, "But, our world is far from that." He leaned back and crossed his arms across his chest, "I hear you're working at a recycling plant now. And how is that going?"

"I volunteer," Albert said, looking at Lord Franklin

with his first glimmer of humility, "You still hear things about me?"

Lord Franklin thawed a bit and uncrossed his arms, "None of us like to speak ill of the dead, Albert. You are in our memories, if not some of our hearts."

Albert could hardly believe his ears, finally some human regard. "I've told you of the visions, the feelings. Something is happening to me, Alistair. Something awful. I can't eat, I can't sleep. I fear for me, my daughter, for others who I can't even see clearly. Something has me in its crosshairs and I don't know why. I've taken this as far as I can, and I need your help." Albert became more intense, almost aggressive, but controlled his voice so as not to attract attention, "Why is this happening? Why me? Why now? I need answers."

"You should know better," scolded Lord Franklin, "Those are the questions of an amateur. You know the truth! There are no answers to 'why'" He motioned to the crowd around them with a flippant wave of his hand, "Everyone thinks there have to be reasons for the unexplained, but we know better. There are no reasons. As the Americans say, 'shit happens.' Well, so does magic! It's natural like fire, or earthquakes, or plagues of locusts. It's the natural order and you either go with the flow, or get out of the way. Something happened to you seven years ago in Los Angeles, and life changed. Something happened to me when I was seven, standing in a fairy ring in the Lake Country, and life changed. And now something has come back for you. Go with the flow, Albert, or get out of the way."

Albert thought hard about what he was hearing, and then asked, "Will you help me?"

Lord Franklin took another deep breath and then slid his right hand forward so that his fingertips came close to Albert's left hand. Albert followed the cue and slid his hand so their fingertips touched. Lord Franklin's eyes rolled up and his head dropped forward so that his blank eyes were looking down at the chessboard. There was a tingling in Albert's fingertips and he caught the flash of a tiny spark as an energy traveled from his lordship's hand into his, and then up his arm. He could not help but close his eyes as he slipped into an altered state.

What came next was what he'd dreaded, yet hoped for. Visions of people, places, and things that had been blurs in his own experience, were now clear and present. He saw his daughter, the familiar surroundings of his work, home, the Holland Park chess patio; and a man eating a sloppy hamburger, talking to a large group of reporters as he licked his fingers and wiped them on an old tweed jacket. He then saw a rapid succession of flashes: red pumps, bloody plastic sheets, teeth lined up in a straight row, and then a strange image from a distance of a woman standing holding two guns outstretched at her sides, keeping two people at bay, looking right, then left, then shooting both of them dead.

With that, Albert's eyes jerked open and Lord Franklin snapped out of his trance. A stronger spark flared as Albert pulled back his hand, and Lord Franklin sat shaking in a sweat. Albert felt like he'd been run over by a bus and wasn't sure he wasn't going to throw up all over the chessboard. The two men just looked at one another. There wasn't much that needed to be said, since they'd both seen the same things.

"Is that what you wanted?" Lord Franklin asked in a weak voice. Albert nodded.

Lord Franklin steadied himself and slowly stood up, using the concrete table as a brace, "Don't ever call me again, Albert. Our debt is paid. I want no part of whatever it is that is about to happen to you." He turned and walked away.

Albert stood up and yelled after him, "You're wrong, you know!"

Lord Franklin turned back, confused, "I beg your pardon?"

"You're wrong," Albert said, "There are three things: go with the flow, get out of the way—or resist."

Lord Franklin shrugged his shoulders, turned and left. Albert sat down, knowing this would not be the last time he would see his old nemesis.

CHAPTER 2

The hotel room was dark, save for a small, flat screen television casting a flickering glow of artificial light in the room. The volume was down, so the only noises to be heard were a wet gagging sound and the rhythmic, audible muttering of a woman. The smell of body odor, pheromones, and stale chips saturated the humid air, and the man and woman in the rickety, creaking bed were oblivious to it all; there were more pressing matters.

Tiffany Bristols, a statuesque, twenty-something call girl straddled the man lying underneath her. The skull and crossbones tattoo on one shoulder blade rippled with the straining muscles below, as she used every ounce of her strength to choke the man beneath her. Sweat ran down her Vogue-perfect face, ruining her mascara and makeup, and her long blonde hair dangled in front of her, covering the face of the man she was strangling. Her muttering grew louder as she strained at her task, "Cum, Jack ... cum, goddamn you ... don't you fucking die on me ..."

Tiffany leaned forward to gain a bit more traction, revealing the face of the man who was gagging in muffled retches. Jack Tate's face was turning blue from lack of oxygen, and his eyes were half-open and watering. Suddenly all tension left his body, and his eyes looked past Tiffany into a blank void. Tiffany saw his pupils dilate and instantly let go of his neck, sitting straight up, "Fuck... Jack?"

No response. Jack just looked off into space, not breathing. "JACK!" she yelled.

Nothing. Tiffany punched Jack in the face with her fist, "JACK!" No reaction. She punched again, "JACK!"

Again, no response, so she slapped his face with both hands as hard as she could, "Goddamn, you son of a bitch, Jack Tate ... I ... knew ... this ... would happen!"

Suddenly, Jack heaved with a huge inhalation of air, knocking Tiffany off him, sending her flying onto the floor beside the bed. Jack sat bolt upright coughing, gagging, and hacking, grabbing his throat. Tiffany jumped to her feet, furious, and slapped him on the back of his head, "Jesus, Tate! Why can't you get laid like normal people? I almost killed you!"

Jack didn't answer, he just got up and grabbed a beer from the little refrigerator by the TV. He looked at himself in the mirror above the dresser.

"Bloody hell ..." he said. His accent revealed his working class roots. His reflection looked empty and lost. The man that looked back at him was one that had seen the worst of the world, but had not given himself over to that world—not yet. He had thick, jet-black hair, typically English pale skin, his body was taut and muscled, filled with a twitchy energy like an animal ready to pounce. Jack wiped away the tears and checked to see how many blood vessels had been lost this time. The whites around his deep-blue irises were infused with countless red capillaries, making his eyes look like the root system of some unseen tree. Chuckling, he thought, *One of these days I'm going to go blind, like my mum said.*

"I'm glad you find this funny. You could be dead ... you punter!" Tiffany looked around for something to throw at him, but Jack shut her down with praise.

"You were brilliant, Tiff. Best yet. You really are developing a knack for this shit."

Tiffany softened a bit, but was still shaken, "I'm

adding another hundred for this one, Tate. Just for scaring the piss out of me."

"Done. Trouser pocket." Jack pointed to his pants, or where he thought he'd left them. He grabbed another beer, plus one for Tiffany, walked over and handed it to her. She guzzled it without a breath, "That's my girl." Jack sat down on the bed, spent, and as Tiffany quickly gathered her clothes and dressed, he tuned out her scolding chatter, and closed his eyes to gather himself, whatever bits were left to gather.

Tiffany broke the moment and threw his pants into his lap. She stood over him with a fistful of pounds, "I'm off." Before he could answer, his cell phone buzzed with a text message. He rummaged through his trouser pockets, pulled out his phone and looked at the screen. The message was from Detective Inspector Gabriel:

THE DORCHESTER NOW
WE HAVE ONE 4 U
& NO FOOD THIS TIME

"Shit," said Jack.

DI Thomas Gabriel was Jack's boss, former brother-in-law, and general pain in Jack's ass. He was an upper-class gent all the way. He went to Harrow on his way to Cambridge. Jack knew Gabriel would love nothing better than for him to drive his car off London Bridge with the windows down and his foot duct taped to the gas pedal. But then he would lose his best profiler and "solver of the impossible." That's how the press had referred to Jack when he made a name for himself with his first case, an unworkable tangle of conflicting clues, evidence, and forensics that had tied Gabriel and his "boys" into knots for months, and that Jack untangled only five hours after being called in by Gabriel.

After examining all the physical evidence, the identity of the human animal responsible for slicing and dicing three young girls, and then displaying their skins outside their parents' houses, was as clear to Jack as a cloudless morning. Some called him magical, others lucky, but most just thanked God that there were people in the world who could find and kill the degenerates he created.

As reward, Gabriel posed with Jack for the press, thanked him publicly for his help, and then declined all his expense request and docked Jack's pay for being late for too many meetings. Jack had the reputation for being the last resort, the nuclear option, or as the mates down at Kensington Station like to call him "Gabriel's cowboy." All of this was perfectly okay with Detective

Sergeant Jack Tate; the more he unbalanced Gabriel's apple cart the more he would be left alone. That's how Jack wanted it. He'd set it up that way, and that was how it was going to stay.

Suddenly a blinding light filled the room, as Tiffany opened the door and rushed out. Not even a kiss goodbye. She left the door wide open as she disappeared into the light of day. Jack squinted into the white light. Outside the door, a woman with a bucket of ice walked past just in time to see him naked on the bed. She froze. Jack looked at her for an awkward moment, and then yelled, "Don't just stand there woman—close the bloody door!"

She reached into the room, balancing her ice bucket with packets of junk food, and pulled the door closed without taking her eyes off Jack. Jack got up, finished dressing, tucked his sidearm holster behind his back and clipped it to his belt, and then unruffled his second-hand tweed sport coat. He took great care to make sure the gun didn't show under his coat, as another violation might get him in some real trouble. Gabriel knew Jack illegally carried a firearm, but left the matter alone for reasons only he understood. Jack's "conceal and carry" seemed to be one of the few things the two men could agree upon. Grabbing a handful of day-old chips, he looked back down at his text message, and said out loud, "Dorchester, eh? Damn, I'm hungry."

* * *

Three news vans were already parked at the inter-section of Tilney and Deanery, the two main streets feeding into Dorchester's roundabout, and another was setting up shop in the parking area just in front of the hotel's main entrance. How the hell did they get permission to park there? Several reporters spotted Jack pulling up in his pea-green, 1980 Morris Marina, and scurried to grab a cameraman for an impromptu interview. But, Jack wasn't interested quite yet. He needed more information before he was ready for his close-up, and besides, he hadn't finished his hamburger.

Jack had a love-hate relationship with the press— well, with everyone, actually, but truly with the press. He was a news producer's dream. Jack knew how to deliver the perfect caption line that audiences would remember. He gave lurid details of crime scene events that no self-respecting DS would volunteer out of fear of compromising a case. And his working class "Essex Man" good looks made him accessible and popular with key female demographics. The press loved him, because of all of this, and because they knew he "got it." It was a relationship that bordered on parasitic, but favored the symbiotic. Jack was a media whore, and everyone knew it.

Jack got out of his car, leaving it sitting curbside in front of the Dorchester's main entrance, and flashed his badge to the attendants, warning them, "Do not move this car. Got that?" They nodded meekly and let him pass without even asking for his keys. He ran inside just as the news crews swarmed his car, only to back off disappointed, like a receding tide.

Inside the hotel lobby, Jack could see the police presence that had preceded him. Tommy, one of Gabriel's "boys," and a crackerjack forensics photographer, spotted Jack and waved him over to the elevators. Jack smiled, took a bite of his burger, and made his way through the crowded lobby.

"Hey Jack," Tommy smiled. Then he looked down at the burger, "You're not bringing that upstairs —right?"

Jack swallowed, "What do you think?"

"I think Gabriel will be happy to see you, that's what I think." Tommy was never good at sucking up, or lying.

"It'll be fine." Jack said.

The elevator opened and two uniformed

Metropolitan police stepped out, spotting Jack, his burger, and Tommy, and with sneers on their faces bumped hard into both, forcing Tommy to take a step back to regain his balance.

"I have to remember not to stand so close to you," Tommy said, following Jack and the trail of his secret sauce onto the elevator.

CHAPTER 3

The elevator opened and Jack and Tommy exited into a throng of police officers, detectives, and forensics people all busy dusting, photographing, and interviewing chambermaids and bellboys. Jack took a nibble of his half-eaten burger, and offered a bite to Tommy, who politely refused, "I better get to work. Great seeing you Jack." Jack chuckled to himself as Tommy put as much distance as he could between himself and Detective Sergeant Jack Tate.

Jack didn't have any details about the crime scene, but he assumed that if he'd been called it was nothing less than carnage. Even with no information, he already knew the victim could not have been dead for more than a day, almost certainly less. The human body doesn't start stinking until it's been stewing in its own enzymes and cellular decay for at least 24 to 36 hours, depending on temperature, humidity, and air flow. With roughly 37 trillion bacteria in the human gut, it doesn't take a forensic genius to imagine the biological anarchy that breaks out when the body starts eating itself. But, in a good hotel, with well-sealed doors and windows, well-designed air ducts, good air flow control, and air conditioning in every room, Jack knew that a body might cook in its own juices for quite some time before anyone noticed. Even if they didn't, room service would find the ugly surprise in the morning during normal housekeeping rounds. You can't drop dead in the Dorchester Hotel and remain anonymous for long. In the case of this victim, there was no smell whatsoever in the hallway, and as Jack got closer to the suite's entrance the only smell he could detect in the air was the slight odor of chlorine.

As Jack came to the door, he made uneasy eye contact with the two uniformed Metropolitan police officers standing guard. One of them stopped Jack with an abrupt hand on his shoulder as he passed, "Shoes, Tate." Jack didn't know the guy, And he's giving me attitude? The cop handed Jack a plastic bag. Jack opened it and put on the paper boots. The other guard chimed in, "We've got something Gabriel wanted you to know. We've confiscated the CCTV footage of the surrounding streets, lobby and corridor."

"Won't make any difference" said Jack "The killer knows how to avoid being seen."

"How is that possible? Every inch of London is covered by cameras," one guard snorted.

"I don't know yet. But he managed to be invisible on the other two scenes, so I'm just sayin'. Anyway," Jack looked at the guard that had stopped him, who was now standing in the doorway blocking his way, "I gotta get inside ... if you don't mind." The officer sneered and stepped aside.

As Jack entered the suite, he noticed the spherical wooden "Counting Sheep – Please Do Not Disturb" sign on the door as he entered. One of the officers tipped his black and white checker banded hat, "Don't bollocks this up, Tate."

Jack shot back, "Fuck off!" Not the most mature response, but he was mad. Just once, he wanted to walk onto a crime scene and not end up leaving more pissed-off than he was when he arrived.

Inside, Jack stood still a moment to get his bearings and take in what departments were present, where in the room forensics were focusing their work, and most importantly, who from command was there and needed to be acknowledged. Everyone in the room was covered head to toe in full-body clean suits. Behind him, Jack suddenly felt a looming presence. Still chewing on a piece of his meal, he turned around.

DI Gabriel stood a good two inches taller than Jack. His shock of salt-and-pepper hair, immaculate suit, and ramrod-straight patrician air left no one in doubt he was a Dundee marmalade kind of guy. There was also no doubt about who was in charge of the crime scene. Gabriel knew everyone's jobs, who was a slacker, and who was over-achieving to suck up and win favor. Jack knew Gabriel made it a point to know every team member's strengths, hot buttons, and closet skeletons, including Jack's.

Gabriel didn't waste time saying hello, he just looked at the leftovers of the dripping mess in Jack's hand, "I told you no food. Lose it now, please." There was nothing polite in that "Please." Jack jammed the final morsel into his mouth, nearly choking himself. After a long drawn-out chew, he swallowed, "As you say, Inspector."

Shifting into business mode, Gabriel said, "We have a Jack Tate special here, I'm afraid."

"It'd better be, for you to call me on a Sunday, in the middle of my fucking confession." Jack was one of two people on the planet who could talk to Gabriel this way; Jack had married the other one.

"Sorry, I forgot how dedicated you are to your 'religion.' How many Hail Marys did Cindy Sin make you recite this time? Or is this a Tiffany Bristols day?"

This was a bit too close to the bone, even for Jack, "You can't let go of anything, can you?"

"I'm like an elephant, Jack. I never forget. You should know that." The moment hung thick between them, as an old wound opened ever so slightly.

"So, what have we got?" Jack asked.

"Follow me." Gabriel lead Jack through the busy room toward the bathroom, as Jack took in random details: a pair of men's shoes on the floor; a suit neatly hung on a wall hook complete with tie and shirt, no suitcase visible; a single champagne glass on a table with an open bottle on a high hat stand; a bed still neatly made by housekeeping, including chocolates on the pillows.

Jack sniffed the air. *Still no body smells, not even shit—this is weird.* "Must be nice to be able to afford a place like this for a one-night stand."

"Why do you say one-night stand?" Gabriel asked.

"One pair of shoes, no suitcase, bed not slept in, a single man's suit. No sign of any other person having checked in with him. And only one wine glass. He had a visitor, alright, but not who he was expecting." Jack

39

was getting curious now, "How much does a room like this go for a night? Seven, eight hundred?"

A woman's voice answered from behind him, "Thirty-five hundred, not including VAT, tips, or body bags."

Jack turned to find a woman standing behind him, who like everyone else—except Gabriel and Jack —was completely covered by a mask and coveralls; only her striking green eyes were visible through her plastic goggles. She had only spoken ten words, but Jack sensed something innocent about her. She was out of her element, uneasy, and perhaps a bit too eager. Jack had to admit her penetrating eyes contrasted beautifully with her dark-chocolate skin. As for her nose and mouth, those were hidden under three surgical masks. The woman held a clipboard close to her chest like a shield. Jack couldn't help but wonder if the protection was meant to be against him.

"Detective Sergeant Jack Tate, meet Detective Constable Mae Valentine." Gabriel smiled at Jack, the kind of shit-eating grin someone gives someone else when they are about to screw them with their pants on.

"I prefer Doctor Valentine, actually," Mae corrected.

Jack held back from speaking. He knew where this

was going, and talking would only make it worse —for him.

"Doctor Valentine, please your ..." Gabriel motioned to his mouth.

Mae pulled the masks down off her face, revealing a nose and lips that perfectly complemented the rest of her well-proportioned face.

"Don't do this, Inspector." Jack took his stand with as few words as possible, but Gabriel was not going to be stopped, and he knew it. "Jack, Doctor Valentine is going to help us all on this one."

If it was possible to have a dead space in a room filled with noise and activity, then Jack was standing in it, "And by us you mean ..."

"You. I mean you." Gabriel replied.

"No." Jack said, looking directly at Mae, not at Gabriel.

"I know she doesn't have your experience with sexual homicide, but she's on the forefront of forensic psychology. Her skillset will be invaluable." Gabriel was being very collegial, no doubt for Mae's benefit.

Mae jumped in, right on cue, "I have my PhD in forensic psychology and physiology from Cambridge. I graduated top of my class at the American FBI Profiling School."

Did she just recite her resumé? Jack looked at Mae

in disbelief, "What?" He then ignored her completely, and gave Gabriel a look of astonishment, "Her skillset?"

Gabriel checked his Pinchbeck-McKinlay watch impatiently, "Doctor Valentine is your partner on this, DS Tate. You will give her every latitude, and you will give me a break. I don't want your usual adolescent caterwauling. It's done. You two are professionals—work it out." He turned to Mae and gave her an order: "Doctor, bring Jack here up to snuff." With that, Gabriel walked out of the room as quickly as he could.

Jack stood dumbfounded, with Mae standing next to him clinging to her clipboard. Jack looked around the room and noticed almost everyone within earshot grinning at his expense, and he was sure he heard more than one chuckle. After a long pause, he finally turned to Mae, "Well?"

"I've been reading the case files. I took the liberty of indexing the suspect-motive matrix to the standard categories: organized, anti-social, disorganized, asocial, gain motivated ... I think this one is some strange hybrid ..." Mae was on a roll that was going nowhere with Jack.

He almost shouted, but kept a lid on it, "Stop!" he said. Jack yanked the clipboard from her hand and waved it in front of her, "This will not work with me.

Just so you know. Don't ever bring a clipboard with you again. Is that clear?" He didn't give her a chance to answer. He handed the clipboard back to her, "Time to check out the meat?"

Mae stuck out her hand for a handshake. Jack snickered at her, "What's this?"

"We've never properly been introduced. I thought we should at least have a civil hello before we see the meat, don't you? Doctor Mae Valentine, I'm your new partner."

Jack looked into her eyes and realized she wasn't going to pull back that hand any time soon. She was trying to make a personal statement. Smart tactics, take the high ground. He licked the fingers that had been holding the hamburger, and then used them to shake her hand. He watched for a reaction. She looked down at their hands, but didn't register any disgust or insult. But, she did return a strong grip that said a lot more than "hello."

"He's in the bathroom." Mae said coolly, and then walked away, wiping her hand quickly on her white overalls. Jack watched her go, and could not stop a little smile.

CHAPTER 4

Two forensics workers were busy in the suite's bathroom when Jack entered. He knew one of them, Monica, a young up-and-comer from the East End, and one of the few staffers who got Jack's gallows humor. The other one was a photographer Jack didn't know, a twenty-something hipster with a clever little sock hat, stylish glasses, and a scarf tastefully wrapped around his neck. Jack hated people who wore scarves indoors.

The victim lay on the floor under a large plastic sheet. There was almost no blood visible through the plastic, and absolutely no blood on the Travertine tile floor. The marble sinks, shower, and standalone bath also looked spotless. The victim was not so spotless, however. Bits of wet flesh stuck to the plastic tarp giving grim impressions of what lay beneath.

Monica was busy swabbing sink tiles and bagging samples, and didn't notice Jack until she looked up to see him touching a set of towels hanging on the wall, "DS Tate."

"Hey, Monica. You alright?" Jack moved over to the next set of towels and felt those, then leaned down to look at the chrome towel holders.

"What did I say I'd do to you if you bollocksed up another crime scene of mine with your fingerprints?" Monica was friendly enough, but Jack knew she was serious.

"Yeah, yeah—promises, promises." He put his hands in his pockets and walked over to get a look at the victim. From behind, Jack heard a gagging sound. He knew who it was.

"Are you telling me you haven't looked at the body yet, Doctor Valentine, PhD?"

Mae stood in the doorway fighting the urge to vomit, "Well, not as such."

"Not as such? What the hell does that mean?" She stared at the carcass and lost a few shades of brown, "Get in here!" He ordered. "I'll just stay outside, if it's all the same."

One of the photographers standing nearby stepped

back a couple paces, "Here comes the pavement pizza!"

Jack could see from Mae's glassy eyes that he was right, "Not on my fucking crime scene she's not." He quickly moved to the doorway, grabbed her arm and spun her around to face the bedroom, just as Mae let go of her lunch all over the rug. The photographer snapped a quick series of shots of her dripping onto the expensive, oriental carpet, and grinned, "Thanks, ma'am."

"If you can't keep it down, then you need to be somewhere else." Jack said.

Mae nodded as she pulled her arm away from him, coughing and gagging. Jack turned back to the bath-room. All eyes were on her as she quickly pulled herself together and followed him.

"How was he when you found him?" Jack asked Monica.

"That's just it. He seems to have been hung from the light fixture, but room service found him on the floor all cut up. And I mean cut," answered Monica.

"So the killer took him down and finished the job on the floor. Looking at the size of the victim here, that couldn't have been easy. This guy must be pretty strong." Jack moved over to the shower. He touched another towel on the rack and then pulled back, looking to see if Monica was watching. No, so he touched them again, "Damp. No visible blood on the glass, or shower floor. Only on the tarp." He leaned in and looked at the shower door glass from an angle, as Mae joined him. He sniffed inside the shower, "You smell that?"

She nodded, "Bleach."

"Bleach! And what does that tell us, Monica?"

"The killer cleaned up," Monica chimed in, without stopping her swabbing and sampling.

Jack turned to Mae, it was time to test her, "And why would a killer risk cleaning up, Doc? The more complicated things get, the more chances of slipping up, leaving evidence. Why not just keep it simple, do the deed, and leave?"

Mae hesitated a bit too long, " ... he wiped down all surfaces with bleach, bath, sinks, shower, everything. He's methodical, had it planned. It wasn't a spur of the moment decision. The victim had a late checkout, so the killer made sure there was time to pay attention to detail."

Jack nodded, "Good, that's the psychology. But, what's the real reason for the clean-up job?"

Mae thought hard, and Jack could almost hear her brain firing, connecting dots, coming to conclusions, "Hemoglobin, and DNA."

Jack smiled at her for the first time, "Bingo." He'd seen many murder scenes where there were no visible signs of blood, where killers had used chlorine to destroy evidence. Fortunately, forensics experts had substances like luminal, or phenolphthalein to show if hemoglobin was present. Bleaching agents like chlorine couldn't destroy all the hemoglobin, so blood could be found, even if a garment was washed a dozen times. But, if the bleach had oxidizers in it, like laundry bleach, then chalk one up for the bad guys; they'd passed their sixth form basic chemistry. The big concern here was not the blood, however, and Jack knew that.

"Which is it, Doc?" Jack held his hand up to Monica, shutting her up before she could speak. From the look on Mae's face he could tell she had also caught on to his little game as well.

"Come again?" Mae asked.

"DNA or hemoglobin? Could be both, I guess. But it's not. Just wondered if you knew which, and why." Jack was really pushing it, and he knew it. Monica and the hipster stopped working to watch the fireworks.

"I'm an expert in people, Detective, not forensics." Her tone was level and professional, but her eyes were gutting him like a fish. Jack didn't back off.

"Yes, I know, the PhD and all. It's just that in this

business you have to be a Jack-of-all-trades to really contribute. Pun intended ... is all I'm saying." Jack turned to Monica, "DNA or hemoglobin, Monica?"

Monica told Jack what he wanted to hear, "Hemoglobin is only an issue if the killer lost blood, and by all signs he was too careful for that. We're not going to find any of his blood. But, he showered and washed off in here, so we might find skin flakes, or hairs and his DNA."

"But ..." Jack walked over to the tarp covering the body.

"But ..." Monica continued, "bleach with oxidizers will destroy blood and DNA, and this guy was too smart to use pure chlorine. He used laundry bleach. So, we're really hashed on this one I think." Then she added her own personal flourish, "And you are a real todger sometimes, Detective."

Jack stood over the body and looked at Monica. She intuitively knew what he wanted; one of the benefits of having worked countless crimes scenes together. Monica searched through her plastic baggies holding bits of tagged evidence, and pulled out a wallet. With her gloved hands she opened the bag and wallet and read, "John Forrest, age fifty-four, five foot eight, two hundred and twenty pounds ..." Jack nodded and she stopped talking. Jack stood in silence looking down at the blank tarp. In the same way Monica knew what Jack wanted, everyone in the room knew this was "a Jack moment," and he needed silence. Mae opened her mouth to speak, but Monica shook her head, Mae needed to shut up.

Suddenly, Jack reached down and pulled back the tarp to reveal the bloody mess beneath, and read the roadmap before them, "A bruise running along the lower part of the jaw on the right side of the face. A circular bruise on the left side of the face, possibly caused by the pressure of fingers. On the left side of the neck, about twenty-five millimeters below the jaw, an incision about one hundred millimeters in length, running right below the ear." Jack lifted the corpse's hands one at a time and examined them, "No defensive wounds"

He walked around the body, "On the same side, but another twenty-five millimeters below, and starting maybe twenty-five more in front of it, is a circular incision, ending about seventy-five millimeters below the right jaw. The large vessels of the neck on both sides are probably severed. The cut is about two hundred millimeters, or so. The cuts were probably caused by a long-bladed knife, moderately sharp, and used with great violence. No blood on the chest, and no visible injuries about the body until just around the lower part of the abdomen. Fifty to seventy-five millimeters from the left side is a wound running in a jagged shape, very deep, and the flesh is cut through. There are several incisions running across the abdomen. There are three or four similar cuts running downwards, on the right side, all caused by a blade used in a downward motion, the injuries being from left to right, possibly indicating a left-handed person. All the cuts were probably done with the same blade."

Jack reached out to Monica, who handed him a plastic glove. He slipped on the glove, leaned down and picked up one of the five teeth lying next to John Forrest's head, and looked at it closely.

"Except the teeth. Those were pulled by pliers, given the marks on the enamel." Jack looked around the room. Everyone was staring at him, a bit unnerved by his savant-like performance, but also impressed.

"Yeah, I'm a todger. But the guy here before me was a bigger todger than I've ever been. Just sayin'." He pulled off the glove and walked over to Mae and handed the tooth and glove to her, "Something you might want to keep in mind."

Mae barely had a chance to respond, before a Met officer interrupted them, "Detective Sergeant, we found something."

Jack and Mae followed the officer into the bedroom

to see several technicians clustered around a bare wall where a large mirror had previously hung. Digital cameras snapped and technicians carefully scraped the wallpaper, gathering samples like archeologists on a dig. One of the techs turned to Jack and stated the obvious, "Looks like we've got a scribbler."

Large red letters were written across the wall:

81808381

WAT GOES ROUND CUMS ROUND
XOXOXO

"Hello." Jack scratched his head and looked at Mae, "You're up." Mae walked up to the wall and leaned in close, "This is what they do."

"Who?" Jack asked.

"Organized anti-social types." Mae got closer and sniffed, "They send messages. The case files said the first two victims had the same phrase, but different numbers." She leaned in closely to look at the lettering, "Someone has a lot to say."

Jack joined her at the wall, "But the other two were done in marker ink. This looks different." He almost touched the lettering. Everyone around him tensed up, and a couple of techs looked like they might jump him to stop him from contaminating the evidence. Jack grinned at their reaction, "What is this stuff?"

Something clicked for Mae, "I know that color!"

"Yeah," Jack said, "red."

"Not just any red, Royal Mandarin." She sniffed the writing again, "I knew I recognized that smell!"

"What the hell are you talking about?"

Mae straightened up and looked satisfied, "lipstick. Expensive. Our he is a she."

"Most serial killers are white males. He could be using lipstick to throw us off the trail." Jack countered.

"Could be," said Mae.

"But you're not sure."

"Hard to say, but ..."

"But what?" Jack actually wanted to know, he wasn't trying to give her a hard time.

"The choice of lipstick. If a guy was just going to throw us off the scent, trying to make us think he was a woman, he'd just go to the store and buy some generic lipstick. But not this guy. He bought an expensive designer brand. Only a woman who knew her makeup would go to that trouble. And not just that. The way this victim was cut up shows a great deal of rage. That fact jumped out at me when I read the case file. All the men have been sliced and diced."

"Go on." Jack said.

"Our suspect is angry. Hateful. Vengeful."

"They usually are."

"This is different."

"How?" Mae hesitated, Jack wanted her to just commit and say her piece, "Dammit, how is this different?"

"She hates men. But not all men. Just a specific type. Maybe a specific individual. Her method looks random, but I'm not sure it is. She's trying to tell us something. Not just with the messages. There's something in her method. I can't put my finger on it."

"Try," Jack demanded.

Mae shifted her weight, then folded her arms across her chest, thought a moment, then unfolded them.

Jack took a deep breath and ran his fingers through his hair in frustration, "A woman who hates men," he said.

"Yeah," Mae responded weakly.

Jack could see she was shutting down, sensing he was about to blow. He didn't disappoint, "Well, case solved! Everyone, arrest every woman you can find because every woman I've ever met sure is a bloody suspect!"

Jack stormed out of the suite. The room burst into

laughter, at Mae's expense. She stormed out after him into the hallway, "DS Tate! Wait."

Jack watched her from the corner of his eye, as Mae quickly removed her clean suit and boots, revealing a conservative, charcoal gray pantsuit, sensible shoes, and shoulder-length, jet-black hair pulled back tight into a frizzy pony tail, making her face easily seen with no distractions. She walked quickly to catch up to him at the elevator, "What the hell was that back there?"

"What?" He asked innocently.

"That was downright mean, and you know it. I don't deserve that!"

Jack pushed the down button for the elevator over and over in frustration, "I'll admit, you did well back there with the lipstick thing," he said, "The rest of your theory is pure conjecture. Or as I like to call it, shite. So let's get one thing straight," he almost punched his index finger into her chest to make his point, "the next time I want a comment from you, I'll ask for it. I ask you a question and you say yes, or you say no. That's it. Understood?

"You did ask!" Mae reminded him.

Jack was caught off-guard. Dammit, she's right. He was saved by a loud ding as the elevator door opened and they stepped inside.

Mae didn't let him off the hook, "I'll take your silence to mean you'll ask my opinion and let me help you with this case.".

Jack looked at her and didn't respond, knowing how she'd take his silence. He saw from her smile she understood. When the elevator opened to the lobby, he and Mae walked to the front entrance to see a throng of reporters with cameras in the driveway.

Mae grabbed a bellboy, "How can we leave the hotel to avoid the press?"

Jack shook his head, "No. I'm going out."

"Gabriel will have your head. He doesn't want any public statements yet."

"Watch and learn." Jack said, walking through the door. The press pounced on him.

"Detective Sergeant Tate—can we get a statement? Is the killing here similar to the other two? Do we have a serial killer on the loose in London?"

Jack pulled a candy bar out of his pocket, opened it up and started to eat it. The press all chuckled, having seen this all before. Jack put on his biggest public relations smile, "Yes."

The reporters clamored and shouted a million questions at once. Jack held up his candy bar to quieten them down, "I have nothing else to tell you, except it's the same pattern as the other two." He looked right into a camera, "And I'll find you, you sick sod. That's a promise."

Mae suddenly pulled him backwards, having come out from the lobby to stop this train wreck from getting worse, "What are you doing? We have to go."

Jack pulled away from her, looking stern, "I want whoever is doing this to know they're not the only one on the hunt. And don't ever do that to me again." Jack walked away back into the pack of reporters.

* * *

A bank of television monitors in a store window showed Jack talking to the press outside the Dorchester Hotel. A woman watched the many screens, the many Jacks, with great interest. A broad hat covered her flowing blonde hair, and she was dressed in a stylish, sleeveless, striped dress, and wore expensive red pumps.

Others gathered around to watch and listen to Jack's impromptu press conference, but she watched with an intensity missing in the faces of the other viewers. She watched as the press talked over one another, how Jack yelled over them, and how a dark-skinned beauty waited in the background, with her arms nervously folded across her chest, no doubt for Jack to be done, and then what? What was next? She knew the answer. As more people crowded around her, she decided to move on, but first she leaned forward and kissed the glass, leaving a bright red smear of lipstick, whispering so only she could hear, "I'll find you too."

CHAPTER 5

Mae Valentine always hoped that when the time came for her to leave this physical world she would be filled with gratitude rather than regret. The way things were going, this wish was looking more and more unlikely. Regrets, she was full of them; gratitude not so much. At least that's how she felt on this night, driving through Golders Green on her way to one of her regrets. Mae chuckled to herself, *No wonder I love Marlowe's Doctor Faustus—that's my life.*

She was headed down Hodford Road, the most expensive part of Golders Green, and an unlikely place to call home for the man she was about to see. She would have thought Chelsea, or Knightsbridge, or even

Highgate would have been his preference. It just goes to show you, books and their covers.

Mae pulled into an upscale building's parking garage and drove directly to concierge parking, there was no other option. She would have to tip big, and she never carried enough cash; another of her regrets. At their first two meetings, they'd always met in public; some expensive restaurant, or bar, and he was never late. Their arrangement was not sexual, or romantic, or anything of the kind; strictly business. But, he was "old school," the gentleman always paid. Mae, of course was not so naive to think this meant there was no price to pay. Her bill was coming, of this fact she had no doubt.

The building's lobby was sparsely decorated: chrome, glass, and stone. Nothing warm-blooded, or earthy, or heartfelt. This was a cold, planned, and calculated world very much like the man who lived here. Checking her scrap of notepaper, she punched the floor number into the electronic pad at the glass-mirrored elevator, and went to the top floor.

She didn't think that a place where people lived could get colder and more uninviting the deeper you moved into it, but that was how this place felt. Mae walked down a long hallway barren of decoration, or architectural flourishes of any kind, and came to a large, gray set of double doors and knocked. It was then she saw the door buzzer and she nervously pushed that too, and waited.

The door opened and Detective Inspector Gabriel stood before her, dressed in the same suit he had worn that day to work. Still on the job. There was a long silence between them and then he half-smiled, "Please come in, Doctor." Thoughts of spiders and flies flashed through her mind as she walked into the apartment, and heard the well-built door close behind her.

The apartment's decor was as cold and sterile as the rest of the building, "I was surprised when you said you wanted to meet here. Why the change?"

He said, "May I take your coat?" Ever the gentleman.

Mae reluctantly took it off.

"I thought it best we keep this private, tonight. Would you like something to drink?"

Mae shook her head.

"As you wish. I will, however, have a drop." Gabriel poured himself some scotch, neat, and motioned for Mae to sit. He took a plain wooden chair directly across from her, as she sat on a minimalist, and incredibly uncomfortable love seat.

"What can I do for you, Inspector?" she asked.

"I heard results were rather mixed today at the

crime scene. Jack put you through your paces, eh?" He watched her like a hawk, or so she felt.

"He's a handful, no doubt. But, I can manage him. I know his type."

Gabriel smiled and sipped his scotch, "And what type is that?"

"Anti-social, narcissistic, obsessive ... probably compulsive, but I haven't seen those symptoms yet. I'll bet we can throw in misogynistic, as well." Mae tried to sound clinical, detached.

"That sounds like many types, not one. Are you sure you can handle him? Our arrangement depends upon it."

Mae shifted uneasily, "Yes, I'm sure." Gabriel didn't answer. He just watched.

"What is it exactly you want me to get from him, a confession?" Gabriel got up and walked to a large wall of floor-to-ceiling windows, with no blinds or curtains. How does he walk around naked? The thought sent a shiver up her spine.

"A confession would be nice, but you'll never get that out of him. No, I don't want anything that grand. I just want to know if you think he did it. Once I know that, I'll take it from there."

Mae thought for a moment, "So you want confirmation, not confession."

Gabriel lifted his glass to her, "Well said, Doctor."

"All I'll have is my gut instinct. There is no more evidence, or data. It's all been picked through years ago. Is my hunch enough?" she asked.

"You're a psychologist, Doctor. Hunches are all you people can ever have. It's not like what you do is real science, after all." Mae felt her blood rush to her face in anger, knowing full well Gabriel could see her reaction. It just spurred him on, "Just because parts of psychology use scientific methods from time to time, doesn't mean the discipline itself is scientific. No, pseudo-scientific at best. But, when the hunches come from the right person, they can be open the doors to real reason and logic, and when there is no more evidence or data, you take what you can get."

Mae swallowed her pride and tried to gain the high ground, "So, you rely on Jack to catch your monsters with his gut, hunches, and neuroses, and now you rely on my pseudoscience to catch him in a lie that you failed to expose—how many years ago?"

Gabriel stood silently, sipping his drink, his eyes bored into her with an almost predatory aggressiveness, "Like I said, you take what you can get. And right now what I have is you. Remember, you came to me, Doctor. You made promises, gave assurances. 'Whatever is necessary' you said. Well, I've done my part.

You have your new assignment. You are on the fast track to a new career. You wanted to be on the front line, not in the background, and now I've put you there. It's time to deliver at your end."

Mae knew she had just been handed her bill, "DS Tate hates me. He won't trust me, he's made that clear. I'm sure he suspects I'm working with you already, he's not stupid. How am I going to get him to open up to me when he barely looks at me?"

Gabriel walked over to a small escritoire and opened a drawer, pulling out a thick file and holding it up, "With this."

Mae walked over to him and took the file, "What's this?"

"My case against DS Tate. Everything he wants to know. All the investigation documents, internal memos, court documents, forensics, depositions— everything. What does a criminal fear more than anything? Leaving a trail of breadcrumbs. What did they forget? What was really known about their crime? Who knew what, and when did they know it? But, most importantly, are they still being investigated, even when the trail officially goes cold? His behavior has gotten even more extreme in the last three years. The isolation, the drugs, the ..."

He hesitated and looked wounded, like a small

child that was about to do something that might get them into trouble, "... prostitutes. He's more vulnerable now than ever before—I can feel it. Those files will tell him he's out of danger. Case closed. This'll put him at ease, prove to him that you have resources he can't get himself. This demonstrates your value as a partner, it's a clear peace offering—and a damned impressive one at that. He won't roll over for you, but he will lighten up and eventually let you in. Then you do whatever it is you do. I get what I want—the man who killed my sister—and you get a bright, shiny new career."

Mae looked at Gabriel for a few moments and then put the file into her purse, "I'll have that drink now."

CHAPTER 6

He arrived early at the wreck that was known as Jack's Kensington Station office. Papers were piled everywhere; heaps of files on all the chairs and desk, candy bar wrappers, fast food bags with half-eaten hamburgers and chips. It was his own personal junkyard. He sat down behind his desk with a cup of tea and a couple of pieces of cold fish wrapped in a paper towel. Not his usual morning fare, but he was in a hurry this morning to get in and start sorting through the forensic reports, and general madness that had resulted from the previous day's crime scene. This last victim was the third in so many months, and Jack knew that thanks to his jumping the public relations gun with his impromptu news conference in front of the Dorchester, that when the team finally had its all-hands meeting to discuss the latest case details, Gabriel would be declaring it official: a serial killer was on the loose in London. Jack was already working on a couple of his own theories, but knowing the size of what was coming next was not something even he would be looking forward to.

Media outlets would have a field day. The twenty-four hour news cycle would be put into overdrive by ratings-hungry news producers scrambling to fill every moment of air space with interviews of retired Scotland Yard Inspectors, forensic specialists looking for their fifteen minutes of fame, survivors of previous serial killer attacks, and endless profiles from psychologists and human behaviorists pontificating on possible killer profiles. Last but not least, the inevitable and soporific Metropolitan Police news conferences supplying a controlled drip of press information about the ongoing investigation. The circus was about to arrive in London, and Jack would be front and center, right along with the dog-faced boy. He took a bite of his cold fish and a sip of Earl Grey, and then looked up to see Mae standing in his doorway.

"I suspect that's a piss-poor breakfast even for you. Back at university I always had a proper fry-up. That was before I became a strict vegetarian, of course." She leaned against the doorjamb.

"Well, I never went to university," he replied.

Mae walked in and looked around for a place to sit down. There was none.

"I'd offer you a seat, but ..."

She stood next to his desk with one hand in the pocket of her jeans, "I figured we got off to a bad start yesterday."

Jack sat back in his creaky chair, "You think?"

"So how about if we try again?" she asked, and gave Jack the file Gabriel had given her.

"What's this?" Jack asked.

"A peace offering. Talk later?" Mae turned and left the office, leaving Jack more than a bit bewildered. Jack put the file on his desk and opened it, and what he saw left him speechless.

* * *

Outside the station, Jack dodged traffic on the busy Earl's Court Road, and caught up with Mae just as she was getting into her car. He grabbed her car door and stopped her from closing it, startling her in the process.

"You scared me to death, what the hell?" She got out of the car, "Can I help you?"

Jack was breathing heavily, trying to catch his breath, "Where did you get this?"

"I see you're one for working out," she said.

Jack was not amused, "Where the fuck did you get this?"

"I have a friend, who has a friend ..."

Jack grabbed her hard by the arm, so she couldn't pull away,

"Your friend has a lot of nerve. And you can tell Gabriel I said so."

"Let go of me, Jack." Mae was clearly not shaken by his anger, and pulled out of his grip, "And don't ever surprise me like that again. Based on the shape you're in I'd have no problem setting you on your bum."

He finally got his breath and stormed away, "Come with me," he said, crossing the road to his Morris Marina, and opening the passenger door.

"Where are we going? She asked.

"To get a proper fry-up."

Mae got into the car, "Okay, but you're buying."

* * *

Jack's favorite restaurant was the unoriginally named "Café America" at the corner of Houndsditch and St. Mary's Axe. Cheaply named, and cheaply decorated, the small American-style diner had the look, feel, and smell of every greasy spoon between Newark, New Jersey, and Fresno, California.

Here, Jack regularly indulged his addiction for sloppy hamburgers, chips, and Coca Cola. Savion Glower, a fat, unsavory, and badly smelling American ex-pat, owned and ran the place, and let out his usual greeting whenever Jack walked in the door, "Jack's back!" All the waitresses and staff let loose ad-hoc wisecracks and insults; clearly this was the ritual for a valued customer.

Mae leaned close to Jack's ear, "How adorable, they love you."

Jack shot her a look, and led her over to "his booth." They took their seats like two gladiators squaring off in the arena. Mae broke Jack's icy glare by picking up a menu and reading, "Well, there's absolutely nothing here I can eat."

"It's food, order something." He pushed his menu to the side. He dropped the file on the table between them, "Gabriel has a lot of nerve giving you this."

Mae didn't react, "I didn't say ..."

"You didn't have to, no one else could have got this information. What's he have on you?" Jack watched as she squirmed a bit.

Gwen, a fifty-something waitress walked over and gave Jack a big smile, "Hello, luv!" She looked at Mae,

"Well, you must be quite a special person. Jackie here never goes Dutch."

"I am special," Mae replied, "But he gets the bill."

Gwen raised her eyebrows a bit, and she turned to Jack, "What'll it be, Detective Sergeant. The usual?"

Jack kept his gaze on Mae, "Yeah. Thanks Gwen."

Gwen turned to Mae, "What about you, sweetheart?"

Mae flipped through the menu, "Do you have anything vegan?" "Sure. Our veggie omelet. Breakfast served all day."

"It has eggs. I'm a real vegan."

Gwen gave Jack a look, as if to say, is this a joke? "No eggs. Okay. How about a nice salad with ham? It doesn't have much meat in it."

"Can I have a plain salad without the ham? And is the dressing non-dairy?" Mae asked.

Gwen was polite, but the strain was showing, "They come prepared from the main kitchen, sweetheart. No ham, no salad."

Jack was amused by all this.

"Oh." Mae turned menu pages, searching.

"You could just pick the ham out of the salad." Surely, this was the answer.

"That won't work. The meat can't touch the veggies. What else do you suggest?"

"How about some nice plain toast?"

"Is it stoneground organic? Or does it have preservatives?"

Jack looked at Gwen, who looked to him for some help. Jack just shrugged.

"I don't bake the stuff myself, luv." Her tone was now getting personal.

Jack broke the logjam, "How about ketchup? It's vegan and it's free."

"Water with lemon. Thanks."

Gwen rolled her eyes at Jack and headed for the kitchen. Jack sat back, surprisingly satisfied by Mae's quirkiness, "I bet you're a fun first date."

"Eating meat is murder."

Jack snorted, "Murder is murder. Eating meat is what makes life worth living."

"Don't you realize you could come back one day as one of those animals you're eating?"

Jack laughed, "What, me a cow? I'm already a horse's ass. Does that count?" Jack watched as she folded her hands in front of her, classic body language for screw you, I'm not going to agree with anything you say.

"It's called karma. Cosmic cause and effect."

"What are you—a Corbynite?"

"No, I'm a Buddhist."

"Jesus. So, are you one of those nuts who throws fake blood on people who wear fur?" Jack was pushing buttons now, just for the fun of it.

"No. I was brought up a vegan. My father taught me that all life is sacred. Especially conscious life."

"Conscious as in twenty-four-seven? Because after five o'clock I'm completely pissed, know what I mean?"

Mae sneered, "Okay. How about anything with a face?"

"Like baby seals and spotted owls and serial killers?" Jack sniped.

"Two out of three, anyway."

Jack couldn't help but smile, "Is that why you went into police work? To protect things with faces?"

"Something wrong with that?"

"No."

"Then what?"

"I guess we may actually have something in common after all." Jack watched as her hands unclasped and she relaxed a bit. Gwen arrived and placed Jack's blood-rare, twenty-two-ounce steak and three runny eggs in front of him. Then she deposited Mae's hot water conspicuously in the middle of the table, dropping one lemon slice into it, "Anything else, luvs?"

Jack gave Gwen a big smile, "I think we're good here, Gwen. Cheers."

Gwen gave Mae a look and then moved on to new customers. Jack cut into his steak and took a huge bite. Blood pooled around the edges of the plate, coloring everything with a light red tint. Mae looked on in disgust, which made Jack savor the moment even more, but there was no avoiding the reason he had brought her here. This file was the last thing he wanted to discuss within earshot of his fellow police, "So, what's Gabriel got on you?"

"Nothing. He just ..."

"If you really read this file ..."

"I did." Mae interrupted.

"... then you'd know that I really hate this bullshit," Jack replied, "So I'll ask again, what does he have on you? Gabriel never does something without an upside for him, and never unless he has someone by the balls." Jack gritted his teeth on the balls reference, for emphasis. If Mae danced on this, he was done with her, so he watched carefully.

"DI Gabriel wants me on this case. It's important to him. It's important to me. I told him the problems we were having. He said he'd fix it and then gave me this. Like I said, I think it's a peace offering."

Jack thought hard before responding, "From who—him or you?

"Both."

"Why?"

"Why, what?"

"Why does DI Gabriel give a shit about you? Who are you?" Jack was actually clueless and wanted an answer.

Mae was silent, then looked off into space to avoid eye contact. Bad sign, thought Jack.

"I saved him from a serious bit of bother on a psych case last year. He promised to pay me back. Now I'm collecting."

"What does that mean? What payback?"

"He knew I was tired of working at the Directorate."

"You're bloody Professional Standards!" If there was any department in the entire structure of the policing establishment of the United Kingdom that was universally hated, it was The Directorate of Professional Standards, or as Jack liked to call them the "Jack Boot Squad." Nothing more incestuous than the police policing the police.

"Former bloody Professional Standards," Mae retorted, "Anyway, I wanted out so I asked him to help me transfer to Serious Crimes, specifically Homicide

Command. To get me on a real case where I could use my talents—my education. I wanted to be in the field. I didn't get into forensic psychology so I could police the police. I'm not political. I hated it! I just want to contribute something. I couldn't do that in the "Jack Boot Squad"—yeah, I know the slang, Jack. I can do that here, with you."

Jack didn't have a quick comeback, which surprised him, "You think you can buy me with this?"

"Buy is such a crude word," she smiled.

Good answer. Jack shook his head, "You break about fifty laws showing me this file and you don't think you're political?"

"Jack, that's everything the department had on you regarding the disappearance of your wife and the case against you—all the internal memos, all the blind alleys. You have to wonder why they dropped the investigation, right? I know we wondered why in the Directorate. Well, you're holding the reason in your hand. They just couldn't prove anything."

"Not guilty is a world apart from innocent. I'm sure Gabriel said that to you—he sure said it enough in my hearing. It's still hanging over me—and Gabriel. In case you hadn't noticed."

"I noticed," she conceded.

"So, you think I owe you something now?"

"Gabriel needs you. I owe him. And now you owe me. Political enough for you?" Jack couldn't help but smile at her boldness, plus she was right.

Mae finished off her glass of hot water and lemon and grimaced, "Ugh, city water." She got up and grabbed her coat, "Remember, all-hands meeting in an hour. Should be fun. See you there—partner?"

Jack put his hand on the file, indicating he wasn't letting it go with her, "Yeah—should be a laugh riot." Mae turned and walked away, as Jack opened the file for another look. It was all there: crime scene pictures, interrogation transcripts, forensics, everything. Gabriel was sending him a message for sure, and his choice of messenger was no less intriguing. He could have just thrown the file on Jack's desk and been done with it, but no, Gabriel packed the communication in a particular wrapper, an annoying, talkative, and aggravating wrapper. *Though this be madness, yet there is method in it*, he mused.

Jack looked down at the file and saw a picture that filled him with conflicting emotions of nostalgia and revulsion. His fifteen-years-younger self stood next to the body of a nine-year-old girl, known to her family as Jane, but known in Jack's world as "victim number three" of the Brixton Flayer, a sick fuck who skinned young children alive and left their skins hanging on the front doors of their parents' flats. Jack had the Flayer to thank for his own meteoric career, and for a life filled with nightmares, cold sweats, and the unshakable belief that every human being on the planet filled one of two functions: to eat or be eaten.

Jack looked at victim number three, and the look on the face of his younger self as he stared down at her raw and bloody corpse, and Jack remembered. He remembered the moment when he chose to eat.

CHAPTER 7

FIFTEEN YEARS EARLIER

The crime scene was newly established, with forensics and senior police staff still on their way. Detective Constable Jack Tate had helped cordon off much of the street, organizing crowd control, and was now doing his best not to lose his mind and rip every senior officer he saw a new asshole. He predicted this would happen, he pleaded for them to listen, he even told them who he thought was the likely target for this new abomination. And, true to form, they ignored him. I should just let them eat shit and die on the next one, because there will be a next one.

As a training Detective, Jack had been given a great deal of latitude by Detective Sergeant Gabriel. He had seen something in Jack from the first day Jack applied for promotion from Constable. Normally, thinking outside the box did not work well in serious investigations, "Follow the protocols, they exist for a reason, Jack," Gabriel kept telling him. The thing was, every time Jack went outside the lines on a case, even the mundane ones, he always came back inside those lines with the break Gabriel needed to get the bad guys, thus making Gabriel and the department look good. And as long as he didn't cross the lines in some public way, Gabriel was happy to hold a long leash.

Jack, however, was well aware that his penchant to go it alone could easily end him back on a street beat, but as long as he pulled off his magic there was nothing to worry about. None of this made Jack popular with his peers, in fact they sniped behind his back and name-called like petulant adolescents, but never to his face of course. That would require a pair of balls. It was all bollocks to Jack, he was getting his, but over time those damn lines got blurrier and blurrier.

After a month as a trainee, Jack just ignored them. He connected the dots faster than any protocol might allow. He followed where the criminals he was hunting led him, and he took what he felt were necessary maneuvers, what many others called unnecessary risks. Verbal warnings were followed by reprimands, which were followed by written warnings, which were followed by suspensions—the result being that Jack found himself tolerated, but marginalized, and only consulted when Gabriel thought it would not make him, or the department, look bad. Jack's career was hanging by a hair and he knew it.

In the period leading up to the Brixton Flayer, all of Jack's cases had been the familiar and common variety; the kinds of crimes you saw on the news any night of the week, but nothing a family couldn't comfortably watch over their toad in the hole with lashings of onion gravy and mushy peas. But, every once in a while God got bored with the common and familiar and sent one of his monsters to Earth to stir things up.

The Flayer was one such monster, and Jack's first bona fide psychopath. For months the body count had slowly ratcheted up, and not just any bodies; nine- to twelve-year-old girls. The victims appeared in various parts of greater London: Chelsea, Camden Town, and Kensington, but the first unlucky girl was found in Brixton, and so the killer's clever moniker, "The Brixton Flayer," was coined.

This beast had a specific appetite and he was getting hungrier as time passed. The local council was in a panic, officials were screaming for police action and results, the Mayor of London was getting daily reports from Gabriel on the investigation's status, and

STEPHEN DAVID BROOKS & JEFF LYONS

political pressure to catch this killer was intensifying by the hour. The stakes were high, and not just for Jack.

Now, with three dead, The Flayer's pattern was well established: kidnap the victim; while she's alive, flay the skin off her body; deposit the skinless corpse in front of the victim's home and attach the skin to the front door (or nearest flat surface); and write the message "take two and call me in the morning" somewhere near the body. The obvious line of investigation was that the killer was a doctor, or medical student, or someone obsessed about doctors, as the reference to "taking two" clearly referred to the old cliché about taking two aspirins and calling the doctor in the morning.

So, all the investigators were focused on medical schools, hospitals, National Health Service offices, and private doctors or medical staff with police records. They were handling this like a brute-force search, as if they turned over enough stones and knocked on enough doors they would uncover the killer. It was only a matter of when, not if. But, Jack knew they were missing the point. They were like the guy who drops his car keys outside in the dark, and then goes over to the street lamp to look for the keys because that's where the light is shining. They were searching in the wrong place, and Jack knew it. He knew it after the first killing. How did he know it? He just knew—as surely as he knew he'd be fired if he kept pressing the point.

None of the Flayer's methodology said, "I'm a doctor." If it said anything, it screamed, "I hate doctors." The Flayer was some twisted soul lashing out and punishing people responsible for some medical travesty. Something was done to him, or someone he knew that resulted in the death of a girl child. A child this monster cared about. Who made the rule that monsters can't love?

Little Jane's body was dumped in the hallway of her parents' second-floor flat, right in front of the door. A forensic tarp covered flesh that was already turning the marbled hues of purple, blue, and green; typical of someone who had been dead for at least twenty-four hours. The child's corpse was giving off the first sickly sweet odors of death and decay. The entire skin of her small body was nailed to the front door, and covered by another tarp. Jane's parents were still inside being interviewed, and prepared for the ordeal of leaving their home and walking past their dead daughter and her pelt hanging from the same door that had previously held the annual Christmas wreath.

Jack stood next to the body with his hands in his

pockets, waiting for the family to leave so he could get inside and look around. Just then, Gabriel stepped up beside him and looked down at the tarp, "Nasty business." He looked to the flat door, "Still inside?"

Jack nodded, "Can I just say ..."

Gabriel shot him an icy look, "The shells under your feet are pretty thin, as it is—don't you think?"

Jack hated Gabriel's threats disguised as patronizing sarcasm. He kept his mouth shut. Just then the door opened slowly and the mother exited the flat with the arm of a departmental social worker wrapped around her. The social worker held the mother's head to help her keep her eyes averted as much as possible. The father was close behind. Both parents looked like they hadn't slept in days, and that the weight of the world was crushing them. Obviously they'd seen the carnage that had been their nine-year-old daughter after the neighbors stumbled upon the scene earlier that day, and screamed like wounded animals until the parents had no choice but to come to the door to see what was happening.

The reports to Jack about what happened next were sketchy, but he had pieced together that all the floor's residents massed outside the flat to gawk, while one neighbor had the presence of mind to whisk both parents back into the flat and then stand guard until the police arrived. It took Jack a few minutes to clear the floor and get control of the scene, but a lot of damage had already been done to the crime scene, what with all the foot traffic and people touching walls and furniture as they jostled to get a view of the gore.

Now the parents made their way through a surreal scene of forensics workers in clean suits, photographers, and uniformed and plain-clothes detectives. As much as they tried to avert their gaze, it was impossible and both parents what was happening to their child, and to them. Jack was unprepared for what happened next.

The mother fixed her eyes on the front door and the tarp that hid its grisly secret. Her legs went weak and she nearly collapsed, only to be caught by the social worker. As the mother gained her balance again, her eyes lifted in what for Jack felt like slow motion. Swollen from crying and crazed with fear, her eyes met his and pierced through him with an intensity that Jack had never felt from the gaze of another human being. He could have sworn he heard her say, "*no love—no mercy.*"

Jack had the distinct sensation of being given a directive. As the parents were quickly ushered away to the elevator, Jack shook his head to re-ground himself. *No love—no mercy* would not be shaken loose, however. The words echoed through his mind, and rather than fade, they became louder and clearer.

He looked around the hallway and watched his fellow police go through their paces: tagging evidence, bagging samples, snapping pictures, interviewing people, doing the same things they did for every killing. They were not going to listen to him, they were going to do what they always did. Jack looked down at the body, then to the bloody door. The last thing he heard as the elevator doors closed on him was Gabriel shouting, "Tate? Where the bloody hell are you?"

* * *

If Gabriel and the hacks at central office had taken the time to listen to Jack, what he would have told them was that the Flayer wasn't done; that he had victim number four already tagged and was moving in for the kill. The next target was probably going to be a ten-year-old girl at the Holloway end of Islington. Her parents were solid working class, a stay-at-home mum, and a lorry driver father who worked for ZP Pharmaceuticals. The dad was a long-term employee of the company, with a well established reputation for working long hours and going the extra mile, literally, to deliver emergency drugs and medical equipment to needy families and demanding physicians.

He was also as corrupt as they come taking bribes, extorting "bonuses" for emergency services, and skimming all the cream off the top of any opportunity thrown his way. The company knew what he was doing, was okay with it, and in fact encouraged it, "Whatever gets the job done" was their philosophy, and looking the other way to give their favorite pet the freedom he needed to exercise his entrepreneurial spirit was completely in line with the company's core values.

Thanks to his own private investigation, it was ZP Pharmaceuticals that gave Jack the breakthrough he needed to piece together the big picture, and zero in on the next likely victim. All three fathers of the victims were directly or indirectly connected to ZP Pharmaceuticals, through a group action lawsuit filed against the company for damages caused by one of its drugs; some arcane chemical compound Jack could never hope to pronounce. The drug was meant to treat childhood depression, but had the unpleasant side effect of blistering the skin. This resulted (in rare cases) in the skin sloughing off in large patches, risking infection and disfigurement.

These facts were certainly worthy of investigation,

and Gabriel's ears actually perked up after Jack had told him of this possible connection to the Flayer, but there was no compelling evidence that the children being killed had any relevant connections to this company, or the drug. Most significantly, autopsies indicated that none of the victims were on drugs or medication of any kind. So, Gabriel told Jack to back off and get with the program, meaning his program.

The lawsuit against ZP involved many people scattered across the United Kingdom and European Union; another argument against the idea that the Flayer was somehow involved with ZP or the case. There was no actionable proof that Brixton was anything more than the first hunting ground for a twisted predator targeting easy prey. All this was true. Jack could not deny the facts. Except there was the problem of the skins. Why skin? Why not cut off limbs? Why not remove eyeballs and fingernails? Why not do a whole host of other unspeakable acts? The answer was obvious to Jack. The Flayer was taking skins because some poor kid lost her's from the drug and had died. Even a first-year cadet would come to this conclusion based on the facts, however circumstantial.

Brixton was ground zero for a serial killer hunting children, because he was acting in a murderous rage to exact retribution for a crime against an innocent. But, the "criminal," in this instance, was a corporation, a nameless, faceless entity with offices all over the world. No, the Brixton Flayer was not lashing out at the evil empire. He was after a specific perpetrator, and all the helpers who participated in making, facilitating, covering up, or expediting the death of a child. This was vigilante justice, pure and simple.

It was a simple matter of basic investigation that led Jack to find the spokes of the wheel that connected to the hub named Doctor Ali Nouri. He was a Brixton-based, Iranian psychiatrist with a reputation for medicating everything that walked into his office, especially with under-the-counter drugs, for ailments not officially sanctioned by the medical establishment. Consequently his services were not covered by the National Health Service, so desperate parents would travel to his Brixton hovel in search of a cure for what ailed their children. And, considering he specialized in the mental disorders of children and adolescents, that meant lots of drugged-out London kids.

In the last year there had been only one patient of Doctor Nouri's that had died: a nine-year-old girl suffering from severe depression. Nouri had prescribed ZP's drug, which he got at a huge discount from the company as an incentive to prescribe at will, and within two weeks of treatment the girl's skin blistered off her body, allowing opportunistic infections to dismantle her immune system and slowly kill her with agonizing complications.

The Flayer, however, didn't start with Doctor Nouri, though Jack had no doubt he would end with him. Better to build the drama by sending a message, "take two and call me in the morning," which was Doctor Nouri's catchphrase whenever he handed someone a prescription. The Flayer decided to pull the spokes off the wheel one by one, starting with the pharmaceutical salesman responsible for selling the drug to Doctor Nouri, then the Pharmacist who renewed the prescriptions, then the landlord who leased offices to Doctor Nouri in exchange for free drugs, and now victim number four, the daughter of the lorry driver who delivered Doctor Nouri's poison at a profit.

There were many other spokes to the wheel: secretaries, delivery boys, nurses, and many other accomplices in the death of this one child so near and dear to the Flayer's heart, but only four of the spokes had one important thing in common. One critical factor united predator and prey: these four all had young, female children. The Flayer would level the field, bring the guilty to their knees, and only after he had taken from them the thing they all held most dear, would he deliver the final blow to the architect of his miserable existence.

Jack saw the progression, the plan, and the intricate and twisted logic that brought him to the one place where he knew the killer would appear, sooner than later: the home of nine-year-old Felicity Jones. Jack had left Gabriel and his team at the crime scene for victim number four, three days ago. He hadn't called in, or given Gabriel his status, or even answered the cell phone that had been vibrating out of its holster.

Jack just waited patiently in the shadows, watching little Felicity come and go with her parents, playing in the street with friends, tailing her to school and music lessons and dental appointments. It didn't matter that this dead silence of his would get him fired, he knew his future was over with Gabriel and the police force. What he had to do now was personal and illegal. But, if his gamble worked, he would have everything he needed to deliver the Brixton Flayer to Gabriel with a big red ribbon on top.

* * *

This brought Jack to Islington, where the presumed next victim lived. On the fourth day of his one-man stakeout, early in the morning, the child left with her mother to walk the three blocks to the bus stop that would take her to school. Jack watched as they walked down the street and then saw a generic, gray Toyota pickup about a street away pull out of a parking spot and slowly move down the street, dew still framing the truck's windshield. As mother and child made their way down the street, the truck inched forward, like a cat stalking a mouse. Jack stayed hidden in his car, watching the dance unfold. From his vantage point he could see all the players of the drama; the bus stop, the targets, and the Toyota. Pulling out a small pair of binoculars he alternated between the mother and child, and the truck. He could not make out the face of the driver, but he was sure who it was. The next bit unfolded quickly, as if well-rehearsed, but nonetheless catching Jack by surprise.

Felicity and her mother sat at the bus stop, as other children and parents arrived. As they sat quietly, the Toyota picked up speed and pulled up directly in front of them. The Flayer, wearing a mask, calmly got out of his truck, walked up to the mother, pulled out a taser gun and dropped her like a sack of flour. Jack no sooner realized what was happening than he ran full speed toward the bus stop. He reached around behind him and pulled his nine millimeter Glockmeister from its holster clip, yelling, "Police—on the ground now!" But the Flayer was one step ahead, having already injected something into the girl's neck. He picked up her limp body and using her as a shield, he quickly climbed back into the driver's side of his truck. Jack reached the vehicle, just as the Flayer pulled away, and just as another car cut him off, giving Jack a chance to grab the door, open it, and level his Glock at the Flayer.

Jack saw an opening and yanked the mask off him. In an instant, Jack got a clear view of the man that had turned the city of London inside out for five months. Average height, receding hair, middle-aged, and ordinary in every way. His face was the kind of face you would forget the moment you saw it in a crowd. Even now, he gave off a pleasant vibe, giving Jack a friendly smile as if to say, "morning neighbor!" as his stun gun shot three-hundred-thousand volts directly into the hand Jack was using to hold the truck door open.

Taser guns were not created equal. Some were better at short bursts on the body's extremities, while others required several seconds of contact with open skin to do the job. The Flayer's choice of gun was below par, fortunately for Jack, who felt a sudden intake of air, as his arms pulled involuntarily into his body. He felt a tightening band connecting his forehead and the base of his neck that forced his shoulders to hunch up to his ears, and then fell backward onto the sidewalk amidst screaming children and parents. The truck sped away and turned the first corner, as Jack struggled to his feet. His hand and arm were numb and buzzing, he was overcome by a deep fatigue, and was barely able to walk back to his car.

As Jack struggled to get feeling back in his body, he got into his car and hoped he had enough muscle control to not kill himself or someone else in an accident. Jack knew he had screwed up. He should have called for help, he should have done it by the book, he should have gone to dental school, and then none of this would be an issue. Shoulda, woulda, coulda. Now it was all on him. Calling in the troops would only get the kid killed. Jack would have to save her and deal with the Flayer all by himself. But first, he'd have to find them.

Jack knew that parents were already describing the Toyota to the authorities on their cellphones, and that there would be an army of police there in short order. He also knew that the Flayer was not going to be stupid and stay in the same car. Jack had to find him quickly before he transferred his booty to another vehicle, and then disappeared into the sea of traffic surrounding them.

A panicked criminal would be running full speed through the streets of London. But, the Flayer was not panicking, quite the opposite. He had calmly tasered a mother and a cop, and kidnapped a young child in broad daylight. He knew what he was about, and this meant there was a change-vehicle parked nearby. Jack turned down the first side street he came to, and looked for an alley. Sure enough, at the far end, the Flayer was moving the unconscious girl to an old VW Bug. Jack held back, knowing the Flayer would lead him to his safe house, or more correctly his killing field. Jack was gambling with Felicity's life, and he knew it.

The chase was more like a crawl though morning traffic, leading into the northeast of London, well into the primary industrial area of Leyton. The Flayer pulled into a small business park off Argyll Avenue and parked his car. Jack watched from the street as his prey stood by his car, looking around slowly for prying eyes. Satisfied he was safely alone, he reached into the passenger door and pulled his sleeping package out, carrying her into a warehouse.

Jack made his way along the side of the building to find an alternate entrance in the form of a broken window. Jack cautiously worked his way into the dark warehouse, coming soon to an open, well-lit workroom. In the center of the room there was a surgical table with a large operating room light hanging over it. Metal tables with an assortment of scalpels and hemostats were close by. The Flayer had made quick work of preparing his victim. Felicity was becoming conscious and was already bound hand and foot by straps to the table. A ball gag was in her mouth, effectively muffling her moans.

Jack was surprised at the cleanliness of the place. This was not a hellhole torture chamber, but rather a well-appointed butcher's shop; from the white tile flooring and gently sloping floors leading to drains, to the three-point lighting system designed to eliminate all shadows in the operating field. Jack was certainly not worried about being overwhelmed physically by this guy, but he had to be careful of more surprises, like the syringes the Flayer used on the girl. Someone this fastidious was sure to have contingency and exit strategies in case of emergencies.

Jack removed his pistol, and raised it to eye level, ready to fire. To his surprise the Flayer turned and looked straight at him. His scalpel was on Felicity's neck, "Put the gun down," he said.

Jack stood still, thought for a moment, and then pointed the gun at the Flayer's right knee and shot. His leg shattered out from under him, he dropped the scalpel, and collapsed to the floor. Jack let out an audible chuckle, well, that was easy. Jack quickly covered the distance between the two of them, and as the Flayer pulled himself up off the floor, Jack hit him hard in the mouth with the stock of his pistol, crashing him back down, "Just stay there, motherfucker!" Jack firmly planted one of his shoes between the Flayer's chin and his chest to press home the point.

Jack picked up a blade to cut the straps off the child's wrists and ankles to free her, but as he did, something stopped him. There was something familiar about the feel of the scalpel in his hand. No love—no mercy. Jack looked at the frightened child on the table, and then down at the killer under his heel, then back to the girl. Terror rippled through him; he didn't see two people, they were just bodies—flesh, bone, blood, nothing else. Like the feel of the heavy steel in his hand, this sensation brought with it vague feelings of nostalgia, longing, an ancient ache.

The Flayer suddenly squirmed and broke the moment for him, and this impudence sent a wave of rage through Jack he could not control. Without a thought or hesitation Jack buried the scalpel in the Flayer's shoulder and cut deep. The Flayer yelped like a wounded dog, and whimpered like the child watching from the surgical table, "Aren't you going to arrest me? Read me my rights?"

Jack didn't answer, he just stood there with his hand on the blade, the Flayer agonizing beneath his foot, blood spilling from the wound and pooling on the floor.

"What are you then? Are you a cop? Or are you a killer?"

From some distant place, Jack listened as the self-talk began. Why did I stab this man? Why don't I pull the blade out? I can slice deeper. I want to slice deeper. Why doesn't this bother me? *No love—no mercy.* There was nothing and no one that could stop him. He could take his time, flay the Flayer, dismember the remains, and then—what? Go have some fish and chips. He did like his chips.

It was as if Jack himself had been pushed off to the side, into some foggy etheric background, while this "other" took the foreground: a stranger, but not strange; a monster, but acceptably monstrous. *I am not a monster. I am not a monster. I am not this thing.* Jack forced himself forward out of the fog to gain some sense of himself again. He was terrified that if he killed the man in front of him, then he would not be able to stop. Would she be next? There was no justice, no right or wrong, there was only an overwhelming urge. Did victim number three's mother sense this in him? Was that why she drilled her plea of vengeance into his soul? In the presence of pure evil, she must have seen the void within Jack that hid this corrupt and debased essence, this mindless and uncensored craving for pain and hurt and hopelessness, this primitive, primeval need to feed.

Jack suddenly felt he was back in his body, returned, and he saw his hand holding the blade above the torso of the prostrate Flayer. Jack's hand shook violently, in fact his entire being vibrated as if the voltage from that stun gun was still flowing through him, head to toe. He collapsed to his knees and looked over to the terrified child strapped and gagged on the table. Her eyes were locked on his and Jack knew she had no idea if his presence meant life or death.

Out of the void, like a black wind threatening to shroud his world in lightless desolation, Jack heard his own mind scream out, *What the fuck!*

* * *

Jack arrived at the hospital just in time to save the Flayer's miserable life. There would be a trial, after all, and closure for the families, whatever "closure" meant, and at least this one little girl would survive her brush with God's twitchy mood swings.

Jack remembered putting the Flayer into his trunk and wrapping the girl in a blanket and placing her in the back of the car, but he didn't remember driving from the warehouse to the hospital, and certainly didn't remember calling into the station to tell his comrades about his escapades. But, they were there waiting for him when he arrived, Gabriel included.

Jack was the man of the hour; single-handedly he saved the day, along with the jobs of every Inspector, Chief Inspector, and Superintendent above him. Gabriel was all smiles and pats on the back. He acted like he'd been the one who had taken down the Brixton Flayer. Jack was fine with that, as he was still shaking, not visibly but on the inside, to the marrow of his bones. *No love—no mercy* echoed in his head like a tape loop. Felicity's screams and the mental images of her skin pulling away from the flesh of her leg filled his consciousness, and the bone-chilling, primordial sensation of his own cold-blooded urge to finish what the Flayer had started left him lost and bewildered about his own nature. He resolved that these feelings would never be spoken of again. What happened inside himself would be his secret, and hopefully with enough gin, time, and distraction, he would forget. *I'm not a monster, I'm not a monster,* he repeated over and over and over.

Suddenly, Gabriel's arm surrounded Jack, pulling him close into a hug, "Here's the miracle worker. Have to say Jack, you have a lot of relieved people singing your praises, including the Mayor of London. The Superintendent is on his way down here, right now, to give you the good news. Your application process is getting fast tracked—Jack Tate, Detective Sergeant. Has a nice ring to it. Don't you think?"

I'm not a monster.

"The press is gathering outside. They want a piece of you, so I hope you're ready for your close-up" Gabriel smiled coyly, "You know, you should meet my sister. I think you two might hit it off."

CHAPTER 8

T he all-hands meeting was in progress when Jack entered the Kensington Station conference room. Gabriel was going over basic housekeeping details for newcomers from other departments and London City brass invited for political reasons, which was department-speak for unruffling feathers and covering asses. These meetings were usually closed to need-to-know police staff directly involved in an investigation, but the fires of panic were rising and needed to be quelled.

Jack found his place in the front of the room, where he would do what he always did in these meetings, i.e., make Gabriel look good. No sooner had he planted himself between the tea and the cheap assortment of scones and biscuits, then Mae entered and made her own beeline to the front of the room. She took a seat in the front row and shot Jack a self-conscious glance as she got comfortable. Jack sipped his Earl Grey tea and gnawed on a stale scone as he watched her, wondering what dog and pony show Gabriel had planned.

Gabriel turned his attention from banal introductions, bathroom directions, and parking procedures, to the large monitor at the front of the room and began his presentation.

"As most of you know, this last victim is officially victim number three. As such, we have to classify this as a multiple murder. Most likely a serial killer." He gave Jack a quick, disapproving look, having watched Jack make the pronouncement himself in front of the Dorchester Hotel, then continued, "The press is already barking up that tree, so this has already spun into the twenty-four-seven news cycle. We're doing the usual media relations to control the story, but you all know how that goes. As always, our best defense is the old 'loose lips, sink ships' strategy." Gabriel turned to Jack, "Detective Sergeant Tate, please bring everyone up to speed."

Jack was caught off guard, as he expected Gabriel to wax lyrical, the way he was wont to do whenever there were more than two people in a room. Jack swallowed his mouthful of cake, "Well, victim number one was a James Henry Beale. Local estate agent, rich, and into kink and prostitutes." Jack made a nonchalant scan of the room looking for sneers or chuckles by his peers, as Jack's own sexual appetites were an open secret in the department. To Jack's surprise everyone seemed to be on their best behavior, although Gabriel was watching him as closely as Jack was watching the room. He continued, "Victim number two was William Jackie Leonardo. Owner of several four-star restaurants in London, also rich and even kinkier than James Henry Beale. Both men were married. Both wives had no idea about their husband's extra-curricular activities. We are running down the last victim's cell phone logs, office and home telephones. So far, no obvious connections between the three victims."

Gabriel chimed in, "Differentiators?"

Jack shook his head, "The last victim, John Forrest. Not much on him yet. Corporate solicitor with Freshfields, Bruckhaus, and Deringer, one of London's top firms. Still tracking down his personal background. But, there was a significant change in the killer's method with this last one, compared to the others. He left writing at all the murder scenes. 'Wat goes round, cums round'," he spelled out each letter, one at a time, so there was no misunderstanding, "C-U-M-S ... was written on a wall with marker ink, at all sites except this last one where he used lipstick instead of a marker, and left a string of eleven numbers. The numbers are still being worked on by analysts. The lipstick was a common high-end brand, but there was no DNA available in the samples. We're still working that through as well."

Jack watched as Mae tensed up in her chair, as if she was anticipating what was next. There was a bit of choreography going on, and Jack was not sure for whose benefit, "Detective, you keep saying 'he,' as if you're sure the killer is male. What makes you come to this conclusion?"

All eyes were on Jack, and he realized that he might have just walked right into it, "Statistically it is the most likely scenario. Britain has only had three serial killers who were women. This lipstick thing is a diversion to distract us. Apparently, an effective one."

Gabriel turned to Mae, "You have a different opinion I believe, Doctor?" Jack suddenly realized the point of all this, Gabriel was putting Jack in his place and doing it in a pubic way just to screw with him, and Mae apparently was in on the game. Jack was now officially keeping score.

The entire room shifted attention to Mae as she took the stage. She was even dressed for the part. Where everyone else in the room was wearing plain smart casual, Mae was dressed to the nines in a blue Armani pantsuit, designer shoes, and her hair was pulled back into a business-like bun.

"As the detective said, the speculation now is male or female? Was the lipstick a ruse used by a male killer to throw a red herring into the mix, or is the killer female and now coming out of the closet, so to speak? I think we're dealing with a female serial killer."

Mae swallowed hard and looked around the room, as everyone watched her, especially Jack, "We've had three female killers, that's true—that we know about. Historically speaking, I assure you that number increases considerably. Nevertheless, when you consider all the victims were killed during or after sex, what is unlikely is that they were not killed by a woman. And then there is the lipstick ..."

Mae picked up the remote control for the slideshow presented by Gabriel at the beginning of the meeting. She clicked through to the slides of the first two killings, "Victim number one, ritually butchered, crime scene spotless, all consistent with this last victim, except the writing." She found the slide with the wall markings, "Different numbers, eleven digits, and the same message: 'wat goes round cums round,' but written in black marker ink." She forwarded to the next crime scene, "Victim number two, ritually killed, again spotless crime scene," she moved to the writing on the wall slide, "And more numbers, nine of them, also written in black ink with the same message." She jumped to the last crime, "And then there is our last victim. More numbers, and the writing, but all written in lipstick." She took a long pause as everyone considered the images they'd just seen.

"The killer used a high-end, designer brand, and a color that is anything but generic. Psychologically speaking, a man trying to hide his tracks would simply have bought a cheap, generic red lipstick and be done with it. He wouldn't have taken the trouble to find an obscure and expensive brand. She used this lipstick, or had extra ones lying around that she could use for writing her messages to the police."

Jack snorted his disapproval for the whole room to hear. His rudeness only made Mae more entrenched, "Everything about this behavior says female, not male. And then there is the sex itself."

Gabriel nodded for her to continue, "What about the sex itself, Doctor?"

"It appears all the victims were into edge play."

Gabriel noticed Jack's reaction and looked straight at him as he spoke to Mae, "Edge play?" Jack looked off in the distance to avoid any eye contact with anyone.

"Yes, suspension bondage, electrocution, cutting,

piercing, branding, enemas, water sports, coprophilia ... that's an abnormal pleasure in feces and defecation."

Gabriel interrupted her, "We get the idea Doctor, continue."

"Yes, well, these three men seem to have been into asphyxiophilia, or erotic strangulation. Usually it's the men who get off choking the women. But these men liked the role reversal."

A cop in the front row asked what everyone was thinking, "What's with the strangulation thing?"

"It's about power, control, but also arousal. For men who like to be the passive partner, the issue is more complicated with power. It's like with dominatrices, men often want to be humiliated or made vulnerable. Ironically, it's usually men who are very dominant and powerful in their own lives, but during sex they want to be submissive as an escape from the crushing responsibilities of life, jobs, or marriages. There is actually a direct correlation between the degree to which a man will allow himself to be degraded by a dominatrix, or sexual abuser, and his social role as a powerbroker."

Mae noticed Jack, who was visibly uncomfortable with the discussion. She also saw Gabriel watching Jack's reaction, and sensed there was a public slap about to occur, "DS Tate, you have something to add?

Please, share with the group. Sexual homicide is your specialty after all," Gabriel prodded.

Jack stared him down, but refused to take Gabriel's bait. He kept his mouth shut, building tension with every passing moment of silence. Gabriel finally blinked and turned to Mae, "Please go on with your theory Doctor."

She continued, "Oxygen deprivation can cause elevated states of euphoria. A more intense erection. Aside from the adrenaline rush of nearly dying, people have reported having incredibly intense sexual experiences."

Picking his own gauntlet up a second time, Gabriel turned to Jack and threw it down again, "We'll probably want to check all the boutique agencies and see who specializes in this sort of thing. You can make those calls, can't you Jack? Might be nice to catch up with old friends, yes?"

Jack finally pushed back, "No sir, I really can't. Don't stretch our resources thin. This is not some crazed female prostitute, this is some sick bloke with a set of steak knives. I need to focus ..."

Mae interrupted him before Gabriel could, "We don't know what this is yet, Inspector. But, I think we need to leave no stone unturned. Interviewing escorts and agencies could turn up some valuable information.

Something like this can't be good for business, so we could get a lot of eyes working for us, instead of against us." The look on Jack's face made it clear to her that she sounded like Gabriel's lapdog, but she was right, and Jack was wrong—she hoped.

Gabriel leveled his eyes at Jack, and gave him no choice, "I agree."

Even Mae could feel the heat of Jack's rage that rose off him in a bilious silence. Gabriel turned to the group, "Okay. Anything else?" No response, "That's all. Stay on it. Dismissed."

Mae suddenly raised her voice to get everyone's attention, especially Jack's, "Excuse me!"

"Doctor Valentine? You have something else?" Gabriel asked. "Doesn't anyone find it odd?"

Jack snickered, "Everything about this is odd."

Gabriel cut him off, "Speak your mind, Doctor."

Mae picked up a folder and read from a sheet of paper, "James Henry Beale, William Jackie Leonardo, John Forrest ..." she put down the folder, "They all have the same nickname." Mae had everyone's attention.

Jack looked at her quizzically, "Nickname?"

Mae looked at him, "One way or another, all the victims are called Jack."

Everybody looked at Jack, who involuntarily

stepped back as if some klieg light had suddenly been shone into his eyes.

Gabriel appeared honestly surprised, "Well, now that you mention it, that is odd." He looked directly at Jack, "And how is it nobody else noticed this two murders ago?"

Mae knew Jack must have felt like kicking himself for missing this obvious connection. He wasn't even bothering to look at her at this point.

"Thank you Doctor," Gabriel said. "Please follow up this new info and see where it leads. That is all."

As Mae picked up her things to leave, she rushed to follow Jack out of the room. He just kept walking, and Mae had to quicken her step to even keep up, "Wait, Jack!"

He stopped and turned, "What!"

"Look, I was just doing my job. DI Gabriel ..."

Jack stepped closer, throwing her off guard, almost knocking her into the bulletin board against the wall, "Your job, PhD, is to have my back. I'm your partner. I'm the bloke teaching you the ropes. I'm the one who will keep you from the tall grass. And you just threw me under the bus in there to score points with DI Gabriel."

Mae hesitated a bit too long for someone that was

honestly misunderstood, "I ... disagree with you on this killer thing. Don't have such a thin skin."

Jack smiled broadly, "Thin skin? I'm an old leather boot, lady. And when I step in shit I don't wipe my heel on the other guy's lawn. I know it's a man, not a woman. I feel it. It's called experience. It's like I can reach out and touch this creep. We're being had, and you and Gabriel are going to get someone killed if you don't start listening to me."

Jack stormed away, "And when you see that bulletin board behind you, just remember who has thin skin. If you still feel like doing some police work, I'll be in the car."

Mae hesitated, then turned to look behind her. Officers and staff smiled and laughed amongst themselves. In front of Mae, laid out in graphic detail, was a series of pictures taken the night of the Dorchester Hotel: Mae throwing up on the carpet, Mae dripping with vomit, Mae trying to escape the camera, and a large close-up of her emptied stomach contents on the soiled carpet with a big red arrow pointing to a description, scribbled in red marker ink; "Pizza girl."

Mae stiffened and stood straight, turned on her designer heels, and followed Jack out of the building.

CHAPTER 9

Mae and Jack rode in silence through central London towards the Knightsbridge part of the city. Mae refused to be the one to break the silence, but she was beginning to feel like the petulant spouse in a sordid marital spat. It was more serious than that, she knew. Gabriel had been less than subtle in his favoritism during the all-hands meeting, and their collusion on the sex of the killer was obvious to all. Mae was having her own doubts about just how unwise it might have been to make a deal with this particular devil, but as they say, in for a penny, in for a pound.

May inhaled deeply and gave Jack the high ground, "Where are we going?"

Jack hesitated, glancing at her before answering, "To see one of my special informants."

"Shouldn't we be heading into a less respectable part of London?" She was serious.

"I don't know what your new boyfriend, Gabriel, has told you, but I work both sides of the tracks."

Mae bristled, but she knew she deserved that, "He's not my boyfriend, he's my boss. Oh yeah, he's your boss too." Jack didn't respond, "So, what makes her so special? I'm assuming it's a woman, based on, you know, you."

Jack pulled his car into the concierge parking area of One Hyde Park, one of London's billionaire bling, residential properties. Mae got out of the car, and realized where they were, becoming suddenly aware of how she was dressed. She straightened her suit and smoothed her hair, as if any moment the paparazzi might storm the car.

"Your informant lives here?" she said.

Jack looked up at the wall of glass and chrome that loomed over them, "Yep. Flats start at about twenty million pounds. I think that makes her pretty special, don't you?" Jack flipped his keys to the valets and joked with them, "No scratches this time, boys."

Mae and Jack entered a lobby of polished marble,

mirrors, elegance and stylish chic. In the elevator up to the fourth floor, Mae got the lecture.

"Jacqueline Monet runs all the top escort services in London. She makes a lot of money, but most of it comes from her ex-husband, who I'm pretty sure she had killed when she caught him cheating with three of her best girls—at the same time. The husband was expendable, but the girls are still working—that's how good they are. And that's how bad she is."

"You know that from experience, do you?"

Jack glared at her, "Do not speak. Do not touch anything. And whatever you do, don't let Jacqui get into your head. She's a master, and you will lose. This is the pit viper sneaking up on the mice, so follow my lead."

"What exactly are we here for? What's the point?"

The elevator door opened. Jack hurried out and made a beeline for a large, expensive set of double doors, "We're going to settle this man-woman thing once and for all. If anyone has figured this out, it's Jacquie."

Jack started pounding on the doors with his fist, shouting, "Jacquie—it's Tate! Open up."

"So now is when I stop talking?" Mae asked.

"Now would be good." Jack raised his fist for another

pound, just as the doors swung open. Standing between them was a sixty-something, stately Jamaican woman dripping in Dior couture. Her chiseled features, impeccable skin, and coiffure suggested a woman as concerned with image as with substance. Jacquie made immediate and intense eye contact with Mae, holding her gaze as if burning Mae's face into her memory. Even with all her psychological training, Mae was unprepared for the aggression of this stranger's invasion into her personal space. Mae could not remember a time—ever—when someone had assaulted her without even a touch; nevertheless, she felt as if she'd just been mugged. Jacquie suddenly broke off her gaze and shifted it to Jack.

"Darling Jack!" She threw her arms around him and pulled him into the foyer of her apartment, leaving Mae to close the doors behind them all, "I'd spank you for being so long away, but as I recall, you'd like that." Arm in arm, and all smiles and small talk, Jack and Jacquie walked into a massive living room that overlooked Hyde Park through a floor-to-ceiling wall of glass. Paintings, sculptures, and expensive antiquities filled every wall and covered every table. Mae dutifully followed them, wanting to touch everything, but heeding Jack's warning. Mae stood back quietly watching as Jack tolerated Jacquie's over-the-top display of affection, and as suddenly as it had begun it was over. Jacquie dialed down the kissy-face façade, and was all business. The snake turned once again to Mae, tasting the air with her forked tongue, "And who do we have here, Jack? A new protégée?"

Jack made quick introductions, "Mae Valentine, Jacqueline Monet—Jacquie, Mae. Can I get a drink?" Jack walked over to the bar, clearly having been there many times, and reached behind it, pulling out a bottle of expensive scotch.

"One thing about you, Jacqueline, always the best." He poured himself a glass and didn't offer anything to anyone else. Jack leaned against the bar and watched Mae, as if anticipating what was coming next. Mae could see in his eyes that he had no intention of getting drunk, at least not in her presence. He was relaxed and giving off the vibe of "unofficial visit" as strongly as possible, while being fully in work mode. Mae was beginning to feel like bait, rather than protégée.

Jacquie ambled over to Mae and offered a handshake, "I am charmed to meet you, my dear."

Mae took her hand, "The pleasure is mine." She could not help but look at Jack for direction, each furtive glance to him being noticed by Jacquie. When Mae tried to release the handshake, Jacquie would not let go.

Instead she lifted Mae's arm up and then stepped

back to give her the once-over, "Let's see—Armani suit, Jimmy Choo shoes. Gucci, Chanel, Valentino accessories. Not real couture, but high-end, store bought. Hmm, Dover Street Market? No, of course not. Fenwick? No. Harrods? I don't think so. Ah, of course, Selfridges? That's the ticket! Even so, expensive, especially on a government salary. Someone's been dipping into the cookie jar—shame, shame." Mae was speechless, Jacquie had nailed the store, and even the part about raiding the cookie jar. In one quick and nimble observation, Mae was reduced to a wannabe clothes horse with social pretensions, far outreaching her civil service status, and bank account. The mugging was complete.

Jacquie released Mae's hand and joined Jack at the bar, "I'll have what you're having, dear."

Jack poured her a scotch, having enjoyed watching the two women spar. Mae almost asked for some water, but realized this was all part of the ritual. No one had offered her a drink for a reason. And Jack was allowing this, maybe as part of some strange initiation, or as some ploy to set Jacquie up for some quid pro quo. Mae knew the smartest thing to do was to do nothing and let the dance unfold. Sure enough, Jacquie took her drink and began moving around the room, like a beautiful, deadly python hypnotizing its prey before swallowing it whole and alive.

"Tell me, Mae dear," Jacquie asked, "Has Jack tried to sleep with you yet?"

Mae looked over to Jack, who just sipped his drink and returned her glance. He said nothing. Mae looked at Jacquie, eye to eye, "Not yet," she replied.

Jacquie let loose a peal of laughter, "Oh, dear boy—try not to get this one killed. She's a keeper."

Jack smiled, "No guarantees."

Tired of being Jacquie's chew toy, Mae decided to step up and ignore Jack's lead, "Ms. Monet, we're here to ask you some questions about some of your staff in relation to the killings that have been taking place in London. I'm sure you've heard about that nasty business."

Jack gave Mae a withering look of disapproval, noticed by Jacquie. Mae continued, "Jack and I have some disagreement about the sex of the killer. Jack seems to think—given your expertise—you can help us. Can you help us?" Mae punctuated the last "help us" with a note of challenge, unmistakably heard by Jacquie.

"Well," Jacquie said, sounding more like a lawyer than a Madam, "What ex*actly* is the nature of the disagreement?"

Mae cut to the chase, "I think the killer is a woman, and Jack thinks it's a man."

Jack finished off his drink in one angry gulp, "I was going to ease into this Jacquie ... you know, more politely."

Jacquie placed herself strategically between Mae and Jack, a position Mae was sure was a conscious choice, "And why not a woman, Jack?" Jacquie said.

"Details on the various victims suggest the killer had to have a lot of upper body strength, the ferocity of the violence is also not typical of female killers. And I just don't bloody think it was a bloody woman—and I know what the fuck I'm talking about, and Mae here doesn't!"

Mae felt Jack's heat and worried that she'd crossed a line, but there was no going back. Jacquie was certainly enjoying the cracks in Jack's armor, though his coarse defiance was clearly unwelcome, "Be careful with your tone, dear, we don't want to start bickering like an old married couple. Someone might say something he'll regret! And then I'll have to ask him to leave."

The three of them stood in an awkward pause that dragged on forever, with Jack and Mae staring down one another, and Jacquie caught in the middle. Jacquie saved Mae from the torture of breaking the silence herself, "Mae, let me guess. It was the lipstick?"

Jack looked at Jacquie with exasperation, "How the hell did you know about that?"

Jacquie ignored him, "I'm right, aren't I?"

"Yes. A man would never have picked that brand or color. He simply wouldn't have known about it. Too expensive, too boutique. And there were other things."

"The sex?" Jacquie looked at Jack as she asked the question. Even Mae was surprised at this, "As a matter of fact, yes." "Edge play, I think that's the clinical term," Jacquie smiled.

"Yes. How did you...? " Mae asked.

"Dear heart, I may live in the clouds, but I assure you I see everything squirming in the mud below." Jacquie's tone turned cold and hard, "Calls are down eighty percent, three quarters of my best women are on the bench. This is all bad for business, and the sooner you find this bitch, the better off we will all be."

Jack smirked, "You're all heart, Jacqueline. Is that all you have? Because I'm still not convinced. Lipstick and panic with your Johns ..."

Mae interrupted him, "Jacks."

"... doesn't mean we're not all being taken for a ride," he concluded.

Jacquie took a long, thoughtful look at Jack, "Is this

really just Jack Tate being the master profiler, or is it you not being able to take being bested by your protégée?"

"Reality is reality," Jack sneered. Mae wanted to slap the smugness right off him, almost as much as she wanted to thank Jacquie for supporting her in this argument.

Jacquie put her hands on her hips and smiled broadly, "Okay, Detective Sergeant. You don't mind if I have someone join us in our little tête-à-tête?"

"What? Yes! I do mind. Who?" Jack was taken completely off guard.

"Brigitte!" Jacquie yelled.

They heard the sound of a door opening and closing down a long, shadowy hallway. Someone was coming. Mae looked at Jack questioningly, she wasn't sure if his face was registering frustration, or recognition. Soon enough, an imposing, majestic redhead emerged from the hallway into the living room. Barefoot, she wore an electric blue, body-hugging mini-skirt that could easily have passed as a second skin. She looked like a supermodel, oozing a primal sexuality and self-assurance, "Yes, ma'am. Do you need me?" Brigitte saw Jack and smiled, "Oh my God, Jack Tate. Been a long time, Jackie."

Jack looked awkwardly at Mae and smiled back,

"Hey, Brigitte. Nice dress." Certainly this was the stupidest thing that could have come out of his mouth. Mae felt sure if he was feeling uneasy, this last fumble left him undone.

Jacquie motioned for Brigitte to come closer. Brigitte obeyed, and as she passed Mae she give her a long, sexy look from head to toe. Jacquie kissed Brigitte on the lips, then whispered into her ear, so that neither Jack nor Mae could hear what was being said. Whatever Jacquie said made Brigitte smile and chuckle to herself.

"Brigitte, why don't you freshen Jack's drink and help him relax." Mae watched as Jack tensed and took a step back in an automatic fear response, "I'm fine, and my drink is fine, thanks."

Brigitte kept coming. She grabbed Jack's glass, along with his hand, and then poured more scotch into his glass. Mae was shocked to see him so out of his element. This cocky, overconfident, know-it-all looked like a small, trapped animal. Jack tried to back away, but Brigitte grabbed his shoulder and then moved around behind him, roughly massaging his shoulders and neck, "Stop it." Jack insisted.

Jacquie watched, not amused or in a cruel way, but like a woman with a point to make.

"Relax, Jack. Remember, I know you like it rough."

Brigitte suddenly wrapped both her arms around him from behind, spilling his drink and dropping his glass onto the oriental rug. Mae stepped forward, unsure where this was going, or what to do. Should she arrest Brigitte for assaulting an officer? Was this just rough play by two women used to being on top?

Jack began wrestling with Brigitte, but found himself lifted off the ground, in a bear hug that left him breathless. In a flash of movement and with no warning, Brigitte spun Jack on his side and then slammed him onto the rug face down, hard. She then pinned his arms behind him and buried her knee in the nape of his neck making it impossible for him to get up. Quickly, she reached behind his coat and pulled out his nine-millimeter pistol and pointed it at Mae, just as Mae was about to lunge to Jack's defense.

Jacquie quickly stepped in as referee, "That's enough, Brigitte. I think we've made the point. Give the policeman back his penis."

Brigitte let go of Jack and moved away, placing the gun on the bar, sitting down on a bar stool with her legs as wide as the dress would allow. Jack got up and looked like he was going to shoot someone. Mae was not sure what was more shocking, that this supermodel trussed him like a calf at a Texas rodeo, or that Jack secretly packed a sidearm, and could so easily be disarmed.

Tucking his shirt back into his pants, and straightening his hair with both hands, Jack picked up his gun and reset the safety, "Nice Jacquie. Nice. We're all friends here, right? Right. Just a little fun." He looked at Mae, "You alright? I'm alright. You alright?" His nervous banter was pitiable, and Mae wanted to tell him it was all going to be okay, but she just answered the question, "I'm fine, Jack."

Jack, shaken and on guard, reholstered his gun, without taking his hand off it, and stepped closer to Mae to create distance between him, Jacquie, and Brigitte. His movement only underscored the true relationship of forces; this was them versus us. For the first time Mae felt that he was taking her side, and actually ready to fight for her.

"Forgive the theatrics, Jack dear, but your old-fashioned sexism is tedious, and in this case expensive!" Jacquie raised her voice for the first time, "I'm bleeding money here, Jack! The only reason for you to come here was to ask me about my girls, because you suspect one. But now I've just proven to you that it could in fact be one of them, because one of them just kicked your ass. Of course this monster is a woman! The village idiot comes to that conclusion before the famous serial killer hunter!" She shook with rage, "If it's one of mine, I want her off the streets!"

Jack pulled himself together and motioned for Mae to head for the door, "Well, Doctor Valentine and I will be going. Thanks for the drink."

Jacquie did not move, but glared at both of them as they let themselves out.

* * *

Mae and Jack sat silently in his car in the parking area outside One Hyde Park. She turned and looked at him. Jack looked down into his lap.

"I know there's a man involved. I know you're right about the woman, but there is a man somewhere in this. I feel him. It's like ..."

"I believe you." Mae said.

"You do?"

"Yes. So, we keep digging. Experience, right? Have to trust the gut." She was throwing him a bone, and he seemed to accept, but she could also see that he was anticipating her next questions.

"Okay, you get this one time. Ask your questions now, because I won't do this again," he said.

"You carry a gun? You know it's illegal, right?"

"Yes and yes. Ask what you really want to know."

Mae let her own judgments drop away, knowing this was the only way to get the truth, "All the women, the prostitutes. Does everyone know? Does Gabriel know?"

"Yes. It's an open secret. They look the other way. Cop culture. Now ask what you want to ask," he said. Mae knew the window into Jack Tate was closing.

"Okay—did your wife know?"

Jack looked at her for several moments, gritting his teeth, then started the car and silently pulled into the traffic.

CHAPTER 10

Albert was at the end of his shift at the East London Community Recycling Partnership in Clapton, and he was ready to go home. He had been a volunteer at the plant for several years, and separating refuse into metals, plastics, glass, and "other" might have been mind-numbing drudgery for regular folk, but Albert found the consistent sameness of the work calming. His mind had been troubled ever since his encounter with Lord Franklin in Holland Park. The images he had experienced that day, and the feelings that had accompanied those images, had stuck with him and grown deeply troublesome. And even now, waiting for his daughter, Mae, to arrive and pick him up, the way she did every Monday through Friday, those feelings were turbulent within him.

In the past, his prescient nature had waxed and waned, like a tide, mostly waning and leaving him alone to appear normal, whatever that was. Those days were gone. Now the battle was daily, the war constant. Albert was losing his psychic grip, and he knew it. Telling the real from the hyperreal had become not only elusive, but maddening. He did fear for his mind, but he feared more for the lives of the innocents, the ones he knew would be caught up in the events that were to come, even as he did not know what events those would be. He saw faces, but mostly they were anonymous blurs. Two stood out, however, Mae and the hamburger-eating sod with the bad clothes and rubbish-bin of a car. He and his daughter had some role to play in the unknown destiny enfolding them, and it filled him with panic that he did not know why.

Albert packed up his backpack and slipped on his favorite old overcoat; the one Mae had thrown away multiple times, and that he, in turn, had retrieved from the charity shop bag. He checked his watch, and saw that it was the appointed time 5:05 p.m. Mae should be waiting at the south corner of the plant.

Outside, he walked down the street and looked for Mae's car, but saw no sign of her. Instead, another car was parked in her spot. Albert could not make out the car, but a man stood next to it, with his back towards Albert. The man seemed to be busy eating something, but it was hard to tell. As Albert got closer, a wave of nausea washed over him. A flood of terror buckled his knees and dropped him to the pavement like a stone. He vomited on the concrete in a loud, wet retch.

The sound of his misery was loud enough for the man by the car to turn and see him on his hands and knees, with vomit dripping from his mouth. Albert wiped his face clear with the sleeve of his coat, thinking now she'll throw the damn coat away for sure. He looked up, the man was walking quickly toward him. It was then Albert saw what the man was eating, a greasy hamburger wrapped in a paper wrapper, drenched in secret sauce. Looking up from the hamburger, Albert saw the man's face, and it was the sod. He looked at the car again, it was the same car from his vision. The more real cannot be denied; events are unfolding.

Albert stood up and cinched his backpack on his shoulder, just as the man reached him.

"You okay, mate?" the man asked.

Albert was silent. He just looked into the man's eyes and felt the wasteland that filled him. How the two of them were connected was a mystery, and one he dreaded discovering.

"That's quite a mess you made. A bit too much hair of the dog, eh?" The man was trying to make light of the situation, Albert got that, but it was pointless. The man reached into his pocket and pulled out several pounds and offered them to Albert, "Here you go. Use this for some food, and skip the midnight train, eh mate?"

Albert refused to take the money, he didn't want to risk touching this person. That would be too much. The man stuffed the bills into a front pocket of Albert's coat, "There you go. Move along now, before some copper kicks your tired ass."

Suddenly, from behind, and what felt like a universe away, Albert heard, "Dad?"

Mae rushed to her father's side and saw the mess on the sidewalk, "Oh my God, Dad, what happened? Are you alright?" "I'm fine. Don't fuss. Where's your car?"

"Well," Mae looked over to the man, sheepishly, "my colleague here, Jack, is our ride. I've had a bit of bother with the car."

Albert looked at Jack with mistrust and then looked at Mae, "Towed again? Or worse, clamped?"

"Clamped." Mae changed the subject, "Detective

Sergeant Jack Tate, this is my father, Albert Valentine."

Jack wiped his non-burger hand on his pants and held it out for a shake, "Yeah, we met," he said. Albert didn't take the hand.

"Can we go?" Albert asked. It was not a question, it was order. He walked past Jack and headed for the car.

"Sorry, he's in a bit of a huff. Just be patient, he'll warm up in the car," Mae said, following her father. Jack threw the remainder of his burger into the gutter, and mumbled, "I'm sure," under his breath.

* * *

As Jack drove, he and Albert stared each other down through the rearview mirror. Mae tried to explain the situation to her father, "Jack drove me to my car and it was clamped. For some reason I parked on the street, instead of in the station lot, and... well, I got clamped."

"My daughter has two master's degrees and a PhD, you would think with all those brains there would be space for remembering to pay parking tickets."

Jack chuckled, "Yeah, you'd think." Mae gave Jack a dirty look, "So, Mae tells me you're retired."

Albert looked out the window, "Did she?"

"So, what did you do?" Albert could see Jack's growing interest. He was not prepared to tell this man too much about himself, until he had a better handle on what role Jack would play in whatever was happening. But, Albert knew he had to give him something, "I was an entertainer."

"That's a pretty broad category. Singer, dancer, actor, bite the heads off chickens at the local fairground?" Jack was pushing Albert's buttons. Somehow this made him less threatening, less inevitable.

Albert smiled, "Geek."

"What?" Jack asked.

"That's what they were called, the people who bit the heads off live chickens. Geeks. It comes from the Gaelic Scot *geck*, and the Dutch or low German *gek* meaning fool. Or those who performed sensationally morbid or disgusting acts. That pretty much sums up my career, wouldn't you say, darling?"

Mae was visibly uncomfortable with the conversation, but didn't challenge him, which drew all the more of Jack's attention. "My father was a magician," Mae blurted out.

"Magic? Oh, I loved that as a kid. Rabbits out of hats, that sort of thing?" Jack pressed on, looking directly at Albert through the mirror.

"Not exactly, Detective." Albert decided to give a

bit more, to test the waters and see what might happen, "More like doves." "Birds? That's all?" Jack's underwhelm was palpable.

"Yeah. Birds. That's all." Albert was disappointed, this was going nowhere; there was no connection. Why was this man now in his life? And why was he with his daughter?

"Sorry, I guess it's one of those things you'd have to see in person."

"Don't worry about it," Albert reassured him, "It's all just three-card Monty anyway, only with birds instead of cards. If you can't impress them with the truth, baffle them with bullshit." Albert knew he was wearing his cynicism on his sleeve, but he didn't care.

Jack's eyes caught Albert's in the mirror, "Were you any good?"

Albert held Jack's eyes with his own and finally got the hit, something clicked. A spark lit where earlier he had only sensed blankness, "Yes. I am—very good." The eyes Albert fixed on grew deep and black, and he felt a presence—beyond the man in the mirror, someone was looking back.

Albert broke away his gaze, "And what is it you do, Jack? What are you doing with my daughter?"

Mae broke in, "Jack and I are working on a case

together." "I'm sure you've seen it on the telly," Jack quipped.

"I don't watch television. I'm not very up on news. Do tell." Albert watched as Jack and Mae exchange knowing looks, unsure of how much to share, or who should share it. Finally Mae nodded to Jack.

"Someone is gutting well-to-do gents in some of the best hotels in London, and your daughter is helping me catch them."

"Her," Albert blurted, "It's a woman. But you know that." Jack swerved the car to the curb and slammed on the brakes. He turned around to confront Albert, "What did you say?"

"The killer is a woman."

Jack looked at Mae a little dumfounded, and more than a little pissed, "Yeah, three's the charm, I guess. I'm finally getting the message."

"Three's the charm?" Albert had no idea what this meant. "Never mind," Jack said. "How do you know this, Mr. Valentine?" Jack made the obvious connection, "Have you two been ..."

"Jack!" Mae sat up indignantly at the suggestion.

Now Albert's visions were coming together. Murder, teeth lined in a row, images of the dead and dying. They were all in it now, up to their chins. And this was Jack's role, he was bringing Albert to the end of things. "No, young man. My daughter does not discuss her work with me. She is a professional. How did I know? Let's just say that doves—well, they were only part of my day job."

The long silence that filled the car made even Albert uneasy. "You're a psychic—a real one?" Jack sounded honestly surprised.

"Believe, don't believe, it's entirely up to you. But ..." Albert debated for a moment whether to share the next bit "... the killer... she's talking to you. Only you. And she's not done."

Mae and Jack gave Albert a look of astonishment. Mae especially looked concerned for her father. He had just shown his hand, sending the clear message to her that he was linked to these events in some way. Now was not the time or place for explanations, Albert knew that. But soon, it would be inevitable.

"Thank you, Detective. We're just on the other side of that corner, we can walk from here."

Jack opened his mouth, hardly ready to let this go, but Mae shook her head at him, "Thanks Jack. See you tomorrow."

Albert and Mae got out of the car, and Albert pulled her away from the car to start walking home. Mae looked back, as if to apologize to Jack for the weirdness that had just occurred. She would have a lot to explain in the morning. Albert looked straight ahead as he walked. It was only as Jack sped past in his car that the two of them made eye contact again, and in that moment, from behind Jack's eyes, Albert heard a voice in his head, *I am Time, grown old to destroy the world.*

CHAPTER 11

Namco Funscape was a family-themed amusement venue next to the London Eye, full of interactive games, a laser maze, bowling alley, bumper cars, and karaoke rooms. The perfect place for a fun first date, or a safe afternoon's distraction for youngsters cut loose for the day, while their exhausted parents enjoyed more adult-themed diversions elsewhere. Namco was also a fun place to people-watch, which was exactly the reason why she was there this evening.

Bowling was not remotely her idea of leisure fun, but tonight the Funscape's bowling alley had a different allure. She didn't know who she would find, but the stone told her the next one would be here. The stone was never wrong.

The bowling alley was styled with bright colors of lime green and fluorescent orange. Rows of green patent leather benches separated ten alleys, and curved artfully around a hub of "ball return equipment" where bowlers picked up their balls and took their turns. Each alley was occupied by a family, or a gaggle of primping teenagers punching one another in fun, or posing for the opposite sex.

She sat at the snack counter, where bowling shoes were distributed, and where staff trouble-shot bowling crises that arose, like pins failing to reset, or balls that were eaten by the return mechanism. She set her bag on the counter and reached inside to find the stone. Pulling it reverently from the bag, she unwrapped it from its red velvet case and held it in her hands.

It was made of clear quartz, with some other mineral inclusions, and fitted snugly in the palm of her hand. No more than an inch tall, the circular stone had a hollow center and scattered light, like a diamond. It was known by many names: Adder Stone, Witches' Stone, Serpent's Egg, Milpreve in Cornwall, Glain Neidr in Wales, Adderstanes in the south of Scotland, but she preferred the Gaelic of the northern Scots, Gloine nan Druidh, Druids' Glass. She placed the stone on the counter in full view for anyone to see, and then waited.

People walked by, ogled and commented how beautiful it was, but no one tried to touch it, or come too near. Something in them knew better, and they were wise to listen to their inner voices. Time passed, but she waited patiently. And then, at the corner of her eye, she saw a young girl, no more than twelve or thirteen, standing off to the side of the room, holding her bowling ball at her side and staring over at the stone with wide eyes and an expressionless face. She motioned for the girl to come closer. The girl dropped her bowling ball on the floor and obeyed, taking a seat next to the woman, with the stone on the counter between them.

"It's so beautiful," said the girl.

"Yes," she replied, "Do you recognize it?"

The girl furrowed her brow and put her head to one side, as if remembering, "Yes. I know its name."

She nodded, "Yes. And it knows your name. It remembers you."

The girl smiled and looked up for the first time, into the eyes of the woman, "No way."

"Yes, way." She smiled back, "Do you want to pick it up?"

"May I?" the girl asked.

"Yes, but if you do, everything will change. Are you ready for that?" she asked.

The girl didn't hesitate, and nodded.

"Then pick it up." The woman said.

The girl trembled, and tears came to her eyes as she reached over and picked up the stone. It filled her hand and gave off more light, but not so much as to draw attention to itself. She watched as a panoply of emotion played across the young girl's face: wonder, fear, anger, rage, horror. Memories flowing, the river of time coursing through her soul and spirit bringing gestalts of awareness, whole lifetimes downloaded, as her essence was psychically rewired with the wholeness of who she really was. When it was done, the girl sat, spent with tears and emotion, but she was wide awake for the first time in her life.

She took the stone from the girl's hand and returned it to its velvet case, and wiped the child's tears and straightened her hair. The child's face was still that of a twelve-year-old girl, but her presence was that of an old soul—an angry, vengeful old soul.

It was only now that she was ready to ask, "What's your name?"

The girl took a sad breath, "I ... I ... don't know. I've had so many."

She smiled, "Excellent. We can begin. There is so much to tell you, and so little time. By the way, what's your father's name?"

"Jack? Why?"

The woman nearly laughed out loud, "Because, sweetie, what goes around, comes around."

* * *

To Be Continued in—Jack Be Dead: Retribution

Buy Other Titles Here:

http://www.storygeeks.com

DID YOU LIKE THIS BOOK? THEN, I NEED YOU ...

Without reviews, indie books like this one are almost impossible to market.

If you purchased this book on any of the online book outlets, leaving a review will only take a minute and it will be incredibly helpful to us—and other readers.

The truth is, very few readers leave reviews. Please help us by being the exception.

Thank you in advance!

Jeff & Stephen

FICTION

Jack Be Dead: Revelation (bk #1)

13 Minutes

Terminus Station

NONFICTION

Anatomy of a Premise Line: How to Use Story and Premise Development for Writing Success

Rapid Story Development: How to Use the Enneagram-Story Connection to Become a Master Storyteller

Rapid Story Development: The Storyteller's Toolbox Volume One

RAPID STORY DEVELOPMENT E-BOOK SERIES

#1: Commercial Pace in Fiction and Creative Nonfiction

#2: Bust the Top Ten Creative Writing Myths to Become a Better Writer

#3: Ten Questions Every Writer Needs to Ask Before They Hire a Consultant

#4: Teams and Ensembles: How to Write Stories with Large

Casts

ABOUT THE AUTHORS

STEPHEN DAVID BROOKS

Stephen David Brooks is a former Visual Effects Supervisor turned multi-award-winning screenwriter and director. Stephen's first feature *Heads N Tailz* won the "Audience Award" at the 2005 Dances With Films festival in Los Angeles. Stephen's latest feature *Flytrap* has played five festivals worldwide and won three "best of" awards: "The Remi" from Worldfest Houston, "Best Non-European Independent Feature" from ECU The European Independent Film Festival in Paris, France, the "Special Jury Prize" from the Chelsea Film Festival in New York City, the "Audience Award" at the Culver City Film Festival, and was nominated for five awards at the 8th International Filmmaker Festival of World Cinema, London, including "Best Feature Film" and "Best Screenplay." Visit www.stephendavidbrooks.com.

JEFF LYONS

Jeff Lyons is a published author and story consultant with more than 25 years of experience in the publishing and entertainment industries. He has worked with literally thousands of screenwriters and novelists, including *New York Times* and *USA Today* bestselling authors. His writings on the craft of story-telling can be found in leading trade magazines like *Writer's Digest Magazine*, *Script Magazine*, and *The Writer Magazine,* among others. His book, *Anatomy of a Premise Line: How to Master Premise and Story Development for Writing Success* was published by Focal Press in 2015. Jeff is a popular presenter at leading writing industry trade conferences, and has been invited to present and consult for the annual Producers Guild of America's "Power of Diversity Producers Fellowship Program," as well as for the Film Independent Screenwriting Lab. Jeff lives in Long Beach, California, has one weird cat, and desperately wants a dog. Visit www.jefflyonsbooks.com.

facebook.com/storygeeks

twitter.com/storygeeks

instagram.com/storygeeks

OFFER—ANATOMY OF A PREMISE
LINE

AVAILABLE ON ALL MAJOR ONLINE
BOOKSELLERS

"Every writer on the planet needs coffee, chocolate, and this book!"

— CAROLINE LEAVITT: NEW YORK
TIMES BESTSELLING AUTHOR OF
IS THIS TOMORROW

[SEE NEXT PAGE]